BE MINE

BE MINE

•

JUSTINE WITTICH

AVALON BOOKS
THOMAS BOUREGY AND COMPANY, INC.
401 LAFAYETTE STREET
NEW YORK, NEW YORK 10003

PRINTED IN THE UNITED STATES OF AMERICA
ON ACID-FREE PAPER
BY HADDON CRAFTSMEN, BLOOMSBURG, PENNSYLVANIA

For Mariana—my Super Daughter

Chapter One

"**D**raw me a map, and I'll find the site myself, Mr. . . ." Sabina Hanlon said firmly.

"Just Jonas, ma'am." The gnomelike little man behind the serviceable desk gave it one more try. "Now, Missy, the roads are right bad out there this time of year, and you're an awful little thing and all. . . ."

"And I'd be better off waiting here until Mr. Peters returns at noon. *If* he returns. You've already told me that." There was little point in taking her anger out on the little man; he'd been left to do the dirty work. So far, Sabina had controlled her temper, but she was reaching flash point.

Keeping her voice silky, she pointed out, "I can't inspect the site from here, can I? Since I'll need Mr. Peters's assistance, it makes sense for me to go where *he* is."

"Well, now, Missy, I'll do the best I can, seein' as you don't know the lay of the land." Tearing a sheet of paper from a tablet, he penciled in their present location, the business office of Calico Mining Company. "It's awful rough out there. You sure you wouldn't just as soon stay here warm and snug?"

Sabina wasn't sure which aggravated her more, his

1

cajoling voice or being addressed as "Missy." "If you don't finish that map right now, I'll fine your boss and this company for obstructing a representative of the state."

This wasn't the first time since she'd begun work as a deputy inspector for the Ohio Department of Natural Resources that Sabina had resorted to threats. Few of the miners took her seriously . . . until after her inspection. Occasionally an owner made the fatal error of offering her a bribe to ignore sloppy mining practices. Sabina wasn't at all offended to know she had become known as "the Tough Broad."

"Here it is, ma'am. You shouldn't have any trouble finding your way, but you'll most likely get stuck."

Sabina took the paper and glanced at it. "I won't have any difficulty. And I never get stuck." She smiled for the first time, and asked, "Is there a decent motel around here? I've not been in this part of the state before."

He grinned foolishly and responded, "None that would be fit for you, Missy. I'll call Miz Kincaid to see if her room's available. She takes in people every now and then. Her house is clean as new paint, and she's a right good cook."

"Lovely. I'll check back this afternoon to see if she has room for me. And thank you." Sabina turned and exited quickly.

She dropped the map on the front seat of the mud-splattered state car. Wrapping the hems of her heavy twill slacks at the ankle, she replaced her dress boots with a steel-toed pair. Next she traded her tailored wool coat for a serviceable quilted jacket. Stepping behind the car, she opened the trunk and removed strap chains, which she attached to the rear wheels. From the corner of her eye, she saw the blinds covering the office window twitch.

Jonas viewed the efficient transformation with dismay. Who'd have thought such a pretty little thing would be so well prepared for the rough country ahead of her? He'd been fooled by the satiny, dark brown hair which curved to hug the fragile line of her chin, by the extravagant sweep of lashes above dark blue eyes, by the misplaced dimple that flashed when she finally smiled.

They'd anticipated an inspection since the first of the year. Industry rumor said the new deputy inspector knew her business, but the workers at the site had been betting against the survival of a female inspector when pitted against Chad Peters. Chad's men had great faith in his way with the ladies. They were confident he could charm her out of taking three whole working days to complete her report. Now Jonas wasn't so sure.

Before the exhaust of the state car dissipated, Jonas pulled the two-way radio from the bottom drawer of the desk. "Tom? The Tough Broad is on her way. Tell Moogie I want to put fifty on the lady inspector.... No, my first bet rides. The odds are goin' to shorten real quick, and I want my backside covered."

* * *

Sabina was grateful for the chains. The car had fish-tailed several times on the way from Columbus, even though the highways appeared clear. Now, faint, early-morning sunlight revealed icy patches on the pavement and highlighted the stark, monochromatic beauty of the rolling southeastern Ohio landscape. The piercing scent of thawed and refrozen earth filtered through her slightly opened window. The sights and sounds said spring . . . even though this morning was still winter.

She was weary of fighting her way over winding, hilly, ice-splattered highways, but the Mozart flowing from her tape deck was calming.

As if by instant replay, yesterday's conversation with her superior flashed through her mind: "Chad Peters might be a little prickly, Sabina. He had a bad experience a year and a half ago."

"What do you mean?" she'd asked.

"Brainard, the man you replaced, offered him a favorable report without an inspection . . . for a bribe."

Righteous indignation shook her. "If Peters bribed him, *he's* dishonest, too."

"Peters didn't pay. Brainard asked for the money up front, and he refused. Brainard wrote him up for three violations . . . without leaving the company office." He paused to relight his pipe. "The fines were processed, but Calico sued. We withdrew the accusations when our own investigation located a reliable witness to the offer."

"But that doesn't mean there aren't any infractions."

"Peters insisted on a full inspection. I did it myself. He was clean as a whistle, but plenty resentful. Said he didn't have the time to play our Mickey Mouse games. Be careful not to rile Peters. He'll be hostile, and he's got a hair-trigger temper."

Sabina willed herself to relax. Chad Peters would have no reason to doubt her honesty; she intended to do a thorough job.

She turned cautiously onto a narrower and less developed road, and ten minutes later sighed with relief as she parked next to a motley collection of pickup trucks and jeeps. The track was suitable only for idiots and miners. "That parking area's going to look like a plowed field before the day's out," she murmured.

In the distance Sabina saw an immense off-the-road truck; several figures stood beside a mammoth front-end loader. She parked her car and set out along a trail which was already a churned mixture of earth and snow. The path ended abruptly just short of a slight rise.

Movement in the cab of the loader drew her attention. As she watched, a tall, muscular figure sprang lithely to the ground. His hard hat dangled from one hand, and early-morning sunlight danced over tousled, sun-streaked blond hair. For the instant he looked in her direction she felt tiny electrical currents skate across the surface of her skin. Then the tanned face turned away. Sabina shook her head to clear it, dismissing the prickle of anticipation as coffee nerves.

Rough, makeshift stairs were cut into the bank. As she approached the first step, a pair of ham-sized hands closed around her waist. Seconds later she was suspended in air, her feet dangling helplessly. "Let me swing you up, little lady," said a coarse voice close to her ear.

A series of vicious kicks to his shins made the giant release his hold. Ignoring the moan of pain echoing in the clear morning air, she climbed the bank, the strap of her bright yellow hard hat in one hand and her clipboard in the other.

At the top she found herself confronted by the tawny-haired worker she had seen moments before. She met his clear, expressionless gaze with a matching lack of animation. A totally irrelevant thought surfaced. *His eyes are the color of country-brewed coffee.* The idiocy of the comparison nearly spawned a giggle, but the coldness in those clear eyes made her wary.

"That man you kicked is limping badly."

The morning sun had no effect on the frost in his even tenor voice, Sabina noted before responding levelly, "Maybe that will teach him to keep his hands to himself. I refuse to be pawed." She shifted her hat to her left hand and extended her right. "Am I correct in assuming you're Chad Peters? I'm Sabina Hanlon from the Department of Natural Resources."

His hand thrust out to grasp hers before Chad realized he'd made the gesture. Even with Jonas's warning, he felt off balance; she wasn't what he'd expected. Then surprise gave way to annoyance. Every spare minute for three days would be spent shepherding this female through his records and over the mine site, where he'd never thought a woman had any business. The scene he'd just witnessed was one reason.

What both disconcerted and annoyed him was the way his whole being was reacting—as if it were radar honing in on a long-awaited signal. He couldn't fathom why. The bulky coat disguised her body, while the loose hood revealed only a finely boned, intense face and amazing deep blue eyes beneath winged brows. Her expression was just short of condemning, proof she wasn't feeling a corresponding response. "I'm Chad Peters," he responded tersely, attempting to control his anger.

"I know you're a busy man, Mr. Peters, but I'm afraid you'll have to make time for me. We have a lot of ground to cover."

Chad nearly smiled a reluctant salute to her direct approach. Her ruthless demolition of Bobbie Russell had his grudging approval, even though he wasn't about to admit it. Still, he resented her presence and the gaping hole it would make in his tight schedule. He mentally shuffled his plans for the week. "You're in the driver's seat, Ms. Hanlon, but I'm pinched for time. We operate well within the law."

"Thank you for telling me. I'm looking forward to seeing the proof," she rejoined, matching his bluntness. "I'll need your help for the next three days. Then I can report your perfection as a matter of record."

"Hey, Chad!" The shout came from the edge of a wall of overburden, material that had been removed to open the seam of coal at the bottom of the excavation a short distance away. He swung his attention from her and moved toward the voice, although part of him was aware she stood looking around her carefully, assessing the extent of the site. Early sunlight revealed the extent of the cut and he saw her move farther away, toward a mound of debris. Suddenly her knees buckled and she sank to her knees, struggling to keep her balance.

Horrified, he broke off his conversation and ran toward her yelling, "Sock, you just cut that out right now!"

His black Labrador retriever had just knocked the legs from beneath the representative of the state. With this humiliation, added to the mauling she'd received earlier, she would have no trouble finding violations that didn't exist.

"I'm sorry, Ms. Hanlon. One of my men taught him that trick, and I haven't been able to break him of it." Keeping his face straight was a struggle. Chad would have given a great deal for a picture of Sabina's face as her knees folded beneath her.

Sensing he was the center of attention, the dog threw himself full length on the ground and pulled his body forward with his front paws, all the while smiling his delight.

Sabina knelt, removing one bulky glove and extending the back of her hand to him. "What a handsome fellow you are!"

The dog nudged his head beneath the slender fingers so she could scratch behind his ears. Chad held his breath, hoping she would smile again, providing him a second glimpse of the misplaced dimple just below the right corner of her mouth. Her tense features had relaxed, and she looked . . . too attractive.

He reminded himself who she was, and why she was here. He kept his voice expressionless as he said, "Whenever you're through playing with the dog, we'll take a look at this schedule of yours."

His words had the desired effect—her smile faded, and as she scrambled to her feet she said coolly, "I have a weakness for Labs, but I hope he doesn't try that trick on me again. I might be closer to the excavation the next time."

"We don't let women get that close, Ms. Hanlon." He realized his words had a double meaning, and wondered if she caught both interpretations.

"You will find I go wherever I feel is necessary, Mr. Peters. Is this all the overburden you have at this point?"

Apparently this inspector did play by the book. She could only be an improvement over his earlier experience, but the timing was bad. Too many problems clawed for his attention. "We're like cats, Ms. Hanlon. We cover each section as soon as the coal is out."

"What a lovely comparison," she responded sweetly. "I'm well aware you don't want any more moisture than necessary to get into the vein. Still, you've been at this site how long?"

"We opened it last month."

She swept her eyes along the wide swath of disturbed earth. "You're working fast."

"It's been too cold to stand around."

"Then I won't waste your time. You're familiar

with an inspection, I'm sure. Tomorrow I want to go over your permits to assure compliance.'' She ran her eyes down the list on her clipboard. ''I also need to look over your last two reclamations.''

Chad stifled a groan and glanced at his watch. ''I can spare the time to take you around part of this site before lunch, but then I have to leave for a meeting. You'll have to make do with my assistant manager this afternoon.''

''I prefer to work only with the individual directly responsible, Mr. Peters.''

He grinned, amused by her starchy reply. ''Then it's a good thing you came early . . . or you might not have caught me at all. Let's go.'' With that he set off at a ground-eating pace.

Sabina was accustomed to clambering over rocks, through mud, and up and down hillsides. Little conversation was necessary, since she knew what she was looking for. Normally, she enjoyed the whole process. Today, for the first time, she had to extend herself. Sure that Chad Peters was deliberately testing her, she allowed herself a grim smile and persevered. The surprised lift of his eyebrows when he discovered her close behind him was satisfying.

Secret amusement gathered inside her as time sped by. He spoke only in answer to her questions, offering nothing extra. If he thought his brusqueness would make her leave before she was finished, she had a surprise for him. ''You don't own Calico Mining, do you, Mr. Peters?''

The coffee-colored eyes darkened and his jaw tightened, then the expression vanished so quickly that Sabina wondered if she had imagined it. "I run the company for the family."

She had no response to such brevity, but wondered what could have happened to cause the pain she had glimpsed. She was unfamiliar with family intricacies. Her own family wasn't close, but she'd discovered in a very short time that in parts of Ohio it was not only close relations who mattered. Shirttail cousins and their connections were considered family, and each member's problems were shared by the others. She thought it unfortunate they didn't feel as strongly about the land as they did about each other. The earth before her was ravaged and bleeding.

The early sun had melted the frost from the banks of clay, from rocks, and from limestone wrenched loose and segregated into anonymous ridges. The very innards of the earth lay revealed.

The sight no longer made her physically sick. She recalled her first sight of an *unreclaimed surface mine,* doublespeak for a strip mine. Tree roots had protruded from the mounds of torn earth flanking a vast, ragged gash. Deep runnels of acid-stained water had eroded each slope. The land had looked as if some immense, clawed monster had made a careless swipe with its paw.

She relived her outrage, then reminded herself that that mine had been in another state. Working in Ohio made her grateful for the tough reclamation policies adopted by the state in 1977.

As she fell back a few paces, her attention fastened

on the lean figure in front of her. Well-worn jeans clung to his legs, causing Sabina's pragmatic side to wonder if he had been able to fit thermal underwear inside such snug denim. Probably not, which could be the reason he set such a brisk pace. Her less practical side was weak enough to savor the view.

A sleeveless down vest concealed the upper part of Chad's body, emphasizing the width of his shoulders. His thick gray chamois shirt made no secret of the strength of his arms.

The response she'd felt when she first spied his figure swinging down from the cab of the massive piece of machinery returned. She'd been struck by a fleeting sense of recognition. She squashed the fanciful thought. Surely that initial awareness was a figment of her imagination.

Chad paused atop a rise, patiently waiting. When she reached his side, she had her first complete overview of the site. They stood at the southern end, the partially mined gash stretching away from them. "This area must have been beautiful once," she said tightly.

"It will be even more beautiful when we're finished."

"Are you telling me you ravage the land and improve on God's handiwork?" Sabina demanded.

"I'm saying we take the bounty nature put here for us and then put the land back in a condition suitable for human use. And frequently we improve the looks. This particular site was an eyesore."

Sabina set her jaw at an angle that mirrored her

antagonist's. "Before you ruined it, this was the way it had been since the age of the glaciers. Future generations should be able to see something that hasn't been dug up, turned over, subdivided, or paved!"

Her voice shook with the force of her emotions, drawing Chad's complete attention. His initial response to her had been a less than pleasant surprise. Since that moment he'd avoided thinking of the lady inspector as a person.

State employees came and went. Some were careless, some were overzealous, while others, he had reason to know, were simply dishonest. None had ever expressed a personal feeling toward what they were doing. He said gently, "You're in the wrong line of work, Ms. Hanlon. You can't become emotionally involved over a piece of land that was nothing but rocks and scrub timber. You'll tear yourself up and burn out."

"I'm not a bleeding heart, Mr. Peters. I just happen to feel the earth has been manhandled enough."

He wanted to groan in frustration. He'd offered sympathetic advice and she'd responded with a blind argument that never failed to inflame him. "Did it ever occur to you that reclaimed land can be more useful, more beautiful? That hundreds of families have roofs over their heads and food to eat because mining provides jobs? Don't condemn an entire industry because of a few careless operators. Some of us love the land as much or more than you do."

"I haven't met anyone like that yet," she spat back, refusing to be pacified.

Chad's temper rose. "You wouldn't recognize him if you did." Her earnestness was at least honest. He turned on his heel, retracing their trail, and threw over his shoulder, "It's time for lunch. You're welcome to eat lunch in the shack with us—if you don't think you'll be contaminated."

Unaccustomed to having someone walk away from an argument about the sensitive subject, Sabina remained in place, still furious, but with no one to vent her anger on. She called after his retreating back, "Thanks for your gracious invitation. I prefer to eat in my car. Alone." Looking down, she discovered Sock poised beside her. He looked from his retreating master to her, as if urging her to follow and apologize.

"Sock!" The angry call confused the animal further, and he whined softly. A second summons prompted another whine, but a shouted "Socrates!" eliminated any indecision. He loped after the receding figure, his head ducked apologetically.

Head high, Sabina followed, maintaining a generous distance from the figures ahead of her. She needed time to cool her temper. During her time with the department, she had yet to see any beautiful reclamation. Nor had she seen land use that showed any signs of creativity. Each site had looked like a sheep which had just been sheared with dull clippers.

A sudden gust of wind penetrated the layers of her clothing, reminding her that she was dawdling. She hurried toward the welcome shelter of her car. The prosaic comfort of the contents of her thermos, a wine-kissed beef soup she'd made over the weekend, would calm her down.

She needed to regroup. Why hadn't her boss warned her that Chad Peters resembled an illustration from a volume of Norse legends? He'd treated her as if his veins were filled with water from a Norwegian fjord— not that she expected anything else. Sabina made a face at herself in the rearview mirror as she settled herself. The man was an enigma, and she had no time in her life for enigmas, no matter how attractive they were.

Chapter Two

The fare in the shack was somewhat rougher, but Chad paid little heed to the knowing smirks he saw on the faces of the men gathered there. Their silence at his entrance indicated a considerable shortening of the odds. The lady from the state had a clear, carrying voice, so her knowledgeable questions and insistence on detail hadn't gone unnoticed by the observant crew. He was also sure their argument had been overheard and duly reported.

"She goin' to find anythin' wrong, Chad?" queried Moogie Burns, a grizzled man in his fifties.

"She'll find we exceed all the standards, just as always." After this morning, he agreed with the scuttlebutt; her knowledge of mining laws and the technical aspects of the industry was excellent.

The men who worked for Calico took pride in their work. Chad knew there wasn't one who cut corners, even during his absence. The betting on the collision of wills between the inspector and Calico's manager offered an entertaining diversion from a winter that had seemed to linger forever. Chad had become aware of a subtle shift in the odds just before the muddy state car had floundered into view.

In spite of his annoyance at Sabina's peremptory manner, her sharp intelligence impressed him. What unnerved him was his instant recall of the way her dark lashes fanned her cheek as she bent over the clipboard she carried, of the throaty timbre of her voice. He had no business noticing the attractiveness of a representative of the state.

"Any word from that foreigner who wants to buy Calico?"

Returning to the present and a change of subject took effort. "Which one? Last time I checked, there were offers from consortiums in three different countries and from an American oil company. They want all the mineral rights they can get, Moogie, and we have a nice selection of contracts in the office files."

He felt every gaze in the shed focused on him. Although he knew they trusted his judgment, each man was aware a change of ownership meant the possibility of layoffs.

"You gonna sell?"

"It's not my decision. Calico and her contracted mineral rights don't belong to me. I'm just the manager." That wasn't the complete truth. He had the authority to sell . . . and occasionally he was tempted. Sometimes he was so tired he could drop.

Chad's thoughts returned to the deputy inspector. He looked forward with great pleasure to showing her his before and after color prints documenting the quilt-like fall color scheme of turning leaves and the summer prairie grasses and spring wildflowers growing on landscapes he and his family had restored, to pointing out the wide-ranging present use of the land.

Chad brooded over his coffee mug, his hands wrapped around it for warmth, unaware that his absorption was causing comment among the crew crowded into the makeshift lunchroom.

"D'you s'pose he's figurin' out a way to do her in?" said the burly dragline operator.

"Naw, he's considerin' how to make a pass without getting kicked in the shins," jibed another. "Figures he don't want to limp the way Bobbie did this morning."

The ribald laughter at Bobbie Russell's expense broke into Chad's reverie, bringing him back to his surroundings in time to hear Bobbie's defensive response to the good-natured ribbing.

"She's a tough one. My shins ache like fire."

"I came close to firing you this morning. When you're on my time, you keep your hands to yourself. What you do after you leave here is your own business," Chad said sternly. "If she gets her back up, she'll find fault where there isn't any. Leave the lady to me. I'll take care of her."

Sabina arrived outside the shack just in time to hear the last sentence. "Take care of me, will he!" she muttered to herself. She hated the chauvinism of the industry. Then out of the blue came a vision of herself with the blond mine manager in a social setting. Her knees went weak. What on earth was wrong with her?

As a gust of wind struck her back, she stiffened and

thrust out her jaw. "We'll see who takes care of whom."

Sabina's peremptory knock on the metal door brought silence within. A silence finally broken by Chad's voice, heavy with command. "Tom, I want Jonas out here by two o'clock."

As the door swung open, Sabina stood her ground, keeping her eyes fixed on a point somewhere beyond Chad's shoulder. "Hadn't we best be getting on with the inspection, Mr. Peters?"

Chad favored her with an equally frigid stare, whistled to the dog, and set out. As if frustrated that he hadn't tired her with the swift pace of the morning's inspection, he walked faster. She could have assured him his unreasonable hope that he could prove she hadn't the stamina for the job was a hollow gesture; instead, she kept up with him uncomplainingly.

"All I see in the topsoil are roots. Where are the trees?"

"We logged before we dug. What good lumber there was was sold, and the rest went as firewood," he replied.

"That took time. Why did you bother?"

"Many people around here still heat with wood. We gave it away," he said with detached amusement. "We have the men and the equipment. 'Waste not, want not,' as my grandmother said."

"Just how many businesses do you run, Mr. Peters?" Sabina asked suspiciously.

"Enough to make a living." He turned to lead the way.

She had no choice but to follow. His lithe movements distracted her, just as they had earlier. Normally, she had no difficulty concentrating on the business at hand. Sabina reconciled herself and enjoyed the view.

"Chad! Ma'am!" The call came from the elfin figure trudging up the slope, and Sabina recognized the rosy cheeks beneath the yellow hard hat as those of the avuncular old man from the mining office.

Chad's voice was bland, as if Sabina were a tiresome duty to be shed. "Jonas will take over, Ms. Hanlon. I can't be late."

Refusing to show how much the casual dismissal annoyed her, Sabina asked neutrally, "Shall I meet you here tomorrow?"

Chad paused in mid stride. "No. I'll see you at the office at eight. You can inspect the paperwork."

He walked swiftly away, and Sock, who obviously knew the source of his nightly meal, followed him.

Though Jonas set a more leisurely pace, he was more loquacious than his boss, and Sabina was exhausted by the time she parked in front of the address the little old man had supplied. At least the house looked welcoming.

His directions hadn't been hard to follow. The little town had only two main streets and one stop light. "A big white house with gingerbread around the porch, just north on Center Street. It's on the left, between two brick houses."

Resting her head on the back of the seat, Sabina

visualized a huge, claw-footed bathtub and a thick layer of jasmine-scented bubbles. She wondered what time her hostess served dinner.

She opened the car door, wrestled her luggage from the trunk, and trudged up the crazy-paving walk. The front door opened before she could pull the burnished brass bell handle.

''My, it's getting cold again. You look tuckered out. What you need is a hot bath before dinner. There's plenty of time.'' Kindly hands pulled Sabina over the doorstep. ''Sit down and take off those muddy boots.'' The thin, graying woman pointed to a gleaming deacon's bench as she closed the door.

Sabina automatically obeyed the brisk command while she attempted to break into the flow of words filling the cozy foyer.

''I was real glad Jonas called about you. Haven't seen a new face around here since Christmas, when my nephew brought a young lady who didn't fit *at all!* He said he was thinkin' of her reputation. Bullfeathers! It was plain as the nose on your face *she* wasn't worrying none.''

Clara Kincaid stopped for breath, dark eyes snapping, and Sabina seized the opening, although she swallowed laughter at the aspersion cast on the unknown nephew's friend. ''This is really very kind of you, Mrs. Kincaid. I'm sorry to be so late.'' She shrugged out of her bulky coat, hanging it on the wooden hanger her hostess produced.

''No problem. I gave up tryin' to eat early like other folk a long time ago. Daniel fiddles around after bas-

ketball practice and Erica's out takin' care of every-
body's business but her own.'' Her capable hands set
the boots aside before Sabina could protest. ''Don't
worry about these none. I'll just clean 'em up for you
when they're dry. Let me show you your room. You're
real private in back. You can come and go as you
please.''

The ''room'' was actually a small, beautifully de-
signed suite. Sabina glanced around the compact sitting room reached through a discreet door set in the
dining room paneling. Mrs. Kincaid's voice flowed
around her. Was her dazed condition the result of exhaustion or the unending chatter of her friendly
hostess?

''There's the bedroom,'' she said, pointing at a lou-
vered door. ''The bath's just off it. There's a no-'count
kitchen, so's you can fix yourself somethin' late at
night, and I put soft drinks and snacks in that little
refrigerator, but you don't have to cook anythin'. I'll
have meals for you.'' She paused, casting a severe
glance around the room as if to be sure it was spotless.

Sabina seized the opening. ''This is so modern. Did
you build this addition so you could take in guests?''

A shadow crossed the older woman's face. ''This
was for me, so's I could be near my son's family and
still come and go like I want to. Zack and Marie died
on the Ohio River five years ago come spring. Their
boat exploded.''

The remembrance stilled the torrent of speech only
momentarily, then she brightened, ''Someone had to
keep a home for the children, so I just moved upstairs.

Seems a shame to let this go to waste, so when there's a need, I take people in. I like to see new faces now and again, and that motel down the road is downright common.''

Sabina congratulated herself for having landed on her feet. Grinning conspiratorily at her hostess, Sabina answered, "I know. I drove past on the way in. Remind me to thank Jonas."

"Hmph! Him. He's gen'rally dumber than most, but at least he had the sense to send you to me. Supper won't be for an hour or so. The twins aren't home yet, and my nephew's goin' to be late. He always is. He'll burn himself out tryin' to do two things at once, but there's no way out of it." She turned abruptly and disappeared through the paneled door.

Sabina swooped up her small case and clothing bag and headed for the bathroom. If she found a stall shower, she knew she would cry from disappointment.

Half an hour later she emerged, rejuvenated by the jasmine-scented water in the capacious white tub. The dark red bathroom carpet pampered her feet and a radiant heater warmed the air.

Warm, clean, and relaxed, Sabina decided the unsettling response she had had to Chad Peters earlier in the day loomed larger in her memory than in reality. The transient nature of her job brought her into contact with strangers every few days. After a night's sleep she would see him as an ordinary man, and the momentary flutter his coffee-colored gaze gave her nerves could be dismissed as a figment of her imagination.

Sabina luxuriated in the slide of lace-trimmed satin

over her skin. She pulled on a softly pleated deep blue wool skirt and matching cashmere sweater over her one feminine vice. If her job required sturdy, practical clothing, she could at least feel a little glamorous underneath it.

As she slipped into narrow matching flats, she reached for her hairbrush to whisk her simple haircut into place. The mirror reminded her that in her preoccupation, she'd forgotten her makeup. Shrugging, Sabina did a rush job with blusher and eye shadow.

"That should do it," she said, grateful her thick lashes passed muster without mascara. She made her way through the small bedroom, stopping only to test the lovely, springy bed with her hand. "I'm going to enjoy you tonight," she promised.

The thump and beat of rock music assaulted her ears as she entered the main house. She followed its compelling rhythm past the oak table set for five, through an old-fashioned arch, and across the hall, where she stopped abruptly, her hand resting on the polished wood of a second oak-framed arch.

As unnatural poses went, the scene in front of her took the prize. An athletically built blond teenager was bent backwards, her hands clasping her ankles while she balanced on her toes. An equally blond young man sketched rapidly on an artist's block.

"Hurry up, Daniel. I'm breaking in half, and I'm afraid he'll catch us," the girl pleaded.

Sabina knelt beside the absorbed artist and peered over his shoulder. The sheet held four other completed drawings—one of the girl standing on her head and three others in equally gymnastic positions. Each mirrored the strength and grace of her young body with minimal strokes of soft lead. The thick pencil moved as an extension of the boy's long, blunt-tipped fingers.

The swiftly moving pencil made one last series of shading. "Done, Eric. You'd better comb your hair. When I'm famous I'll immortalize you in oil . . . only I'll make you look dignified." He noticed his audience belatedly. "Excuse me, ma'am. I didn't hear you come in."

"I didn't want to interrupt genius at work. Those are fantastic drawings. May I look more closely?"

He extended them hesitantly. "Sure." He cast a nervous glance toward the hall before continuing. "You must be the lady from Natural Resources. Gran said you were here. I'm Daniel Kincaid." He rose to his feet.

"And I'm Erica," the girl said.

Sabina looked up, her breath catching as she stared at the tall, golden-haired adolescents. "Viking children," she murmured involuntarily. Daniel's masculine, high-cheekboned face was feminized in his sister, whose head came nearly to his ear. "I'm Sabina Hanlon. I'm sorry I peered over your shoulder, Daniel, but I was fascinated by how quickly you were working."

"I'm glad you didn't interrupt. I was about to die, and I couldn't have matched the pose later," Erica responded. "We wanted to get this done before our cousin gets here. He . . . thinks Daniel takes advantage of me, which of course he doesn't. We're twins, you know."

"I'd sort of guessed that," Sabina said wryly. "I've heard it's impossible for one twin to take advantage of the other." Erica had been about to say something else, then had substituted what sounded like a lame excuse.

Daniel shifted his feet, as self-conscious as it was possible for close to six and a half feet of muscles to look. "This is an art class project: The Unnatural Human Form. Eric is a perfect model." He winced as his sister's elbow connected with his ribs. "I mean, uh, she's almost double-jointed."

"Good recovery, Daniel," Erica teased.

Their exchange amused Sabina, who looked more closely at the sketches. "I'd say you're on your way to an A." She returned the drawing to him. "You'd better put this someplace safe. I'd hate for your sister to have to go through all that again."

More relief than seemed necessary swept over the boy's face as he put the sketches in the window seat. At the sound of the front door opening, Erica murmured, "Just in time." She rushed past Sabina, shrieking, "Chad! You beast, you've been back two whole days and haven't come to see us till now. Why not?"

Sabina turned in time to see the man in the arch brace himself before Erica's strong young arms engulfed him. Before the head of hair much the color of his own obstructed her view of his face, he smiled broadly. Chad Peters was tall, but this Viking girl cousin was just a few inches shorter. She groaned inwardly as Daniel joined the two, muttering to herself, "I should have known. There couldn't be many people in a town this small with lion manes like that. What a fun evening *this* will be."

Three tawny heads turned toward her in unison. She felt left out—not unwelcome, since the twins' smiles were genuine—but an outsider. Chad Peters's expression could only be described as wary, but he managed the greeting with grace. "Ms. Hanlon. I didn't know you were staying here until Aunt Clara told me. I hope you'll be comfortable."

It must have been a whale of an appointment, Sabina decided. In his beautifully tailored, charcoal gray suit he looked as if he had just stepped off Wall Street. A conservative burgundy-and-silver striped tie was half hidden beneath the vest. If he were to model dress shirts, Sabina was sure Chad Peters would cause a run on the market for Arrow. Surprisingly, his *GQ* appearance helped her deal with the jolt of awareness which swept from her head to her toes. "As comfortable as I *can* be, considering that I seem to have taken lodging in the middle of your family."

"Your image doesn't live up to your reputation, Ms. Hanlon."

Sabina nearly flinched under Chad's quick, assessing glance. She knew without words that he was wondering exactly how old she was. Her friends had urged her to wear more sophisticated clothing and an upscale hairstyle, but they didn't match her line of work, and she preferred to let her capability proclaim her maturity.

"If you mean I don't look like a Tough Broad, I'll take that as a compliment." She met his gaze steadily, allowing a flash of humor to acknowledge his reference. "We have a grapevine on our side of the fence too, Mr. Peters."

"*She* can't be the Tough Broad, Chad," protested Daniel. "She's just a little thing." As soon as the words passed his lips, he turned bright scarlet.

His discomfiture was so genuine Sabina grinned at him.

"That 'little thing' left Bobbie Russell limping this morning."

Her eyes dancing with respect, Erica came over to Sabina with her hand outstretched. "Good for you! He's a gross lech. Will you tell me later what you did to him?"

Sabina sensed acceptance by at least two of her dinner companions, but, as they crossed the hall to the dining room, she knew she was safer without Chad Peters's approval. Whatever the man had, he could bottle it, sell it, and make millions. For the first time since her disastrous engagement, she had to remind herself she wasn't in the market.

The aroma of the food on the heavy oak table distracted her, and she filed away her ridiculous worry about a situation that would never occur. *It just goes to show,* she thought as Daniel held her chair for her, *that I'm more interested in food than in men.*

Sabina helped herself to generous portions of baked chicken and golden homemade noodles. As she spooned butternut squash onto her plate, Chad's soft, "Fresh air and exercise certainly make a person hungry, don't they?" reached her ears.

Lowering the utensil, she blushed beneath his amused golden appraisal. He grinned before closing his lips over a small wedge of breast meat and winked mischievously.

"Behave yourself, Chad. You can't tease company like you do family," declared Clara. "The girl has to keep her strength up if she's goin' to tramp all over the county in this weather." She thumped a serving bowl back in its place and changed the subject. "It's a mercy to see you dressed decent for a change. Last time you came, you were mud from head to toe . . . tracked up my kitchen just like you did when you were ten."

Sabina wondered just what kind of a meeting Chad Peters had attended. His jacket hung carelessly on the back of his chair, along with his tie. The vest and the top button of his shirt were undone. He'd removed heavy gold links before turning up his shirt cuffs, and tawny hair curled along his muscular forearms. He looked gorgeous.

She hoped the heat she felt was generated by her recent intake of calories, but a faint voice in the back of her mind graded the hope a one on a scale of ten.

"Did the board vote that loan for the Mourys' addition to the restaurant?" Clara's interruption of Sabina's unnerving thoughts was welcome.

"Now, Aunt Clara. You know I can't tell you. Wait for the morning report from the telephone grapevine." Indulgent amusement laced his voice, but his refusal was definite.

"Well, if the president of the bank can't tell his own

aunt a little thing like that, what's the world comin' to? After all, I knew everythin' about it before the meetin'.''

The smile on Chad's face took Sabina's breath away. Perhaps it was the genuine love and affection in his expression that gave it such power, but her head reeled. If he ever looked at her like that . . .

"Mary Moury told you the plans. Let her tell you the results. I'm sure she'll know more details than I can remember about the proceedings . . . even though she wasn't there.''

The elderly lady gave him a long-suffering look. She was obviously accustomed to being put gently in her place.

Then the full implication of the exchange hit Sabina. She blurted out, ''A bank! I thought you operated a mining company!''

Four pairs of eyes focused on her simultaneously, and three voices were overridden by Chad's. ''I *manage* one, Ms. Hanlon. Or at least I will until Daniel takes over his father's company. My father founded a chain of small banks in this area before he retired, and that's my primary responsibility. I wear two hats.''

Sabina remembered her resentment at being summarily left with Jonas that afternoon, then made the connection, the reason someone had needed to take over Calico. Aware her clumsy question must have reminded Clara and the twins of their loss, she looked across the table. There was sadness in the twins' eyes, but the identical gray gazes held something else— something which vanished quickly.

There was no graceful way to apologize. As she floundered, Chad said gently, "That's why I delegate things, Ms. Hanlon."

Unable to compensate for her blunder, and uneasy with the unexpected warmth in his eyes, she searched for a change of subject. "I'll be much more comfortable if you all call me Sabina. I can't eat at a family table and be Ms.'d to death."

As if grateful for the adept conversational shift, the twins returned their attention to their plates. Chad said, "Fine. You can return the favor by calling me Chad. I always look over my shoulder for my father when someone calls me Mr. Peters."

Warmth still lurked in his eyes, and Sabina lowered her eyes to her plate. She hoped he hadn't noticed the color she felt rising in her cheeks.

Chad and Daniel argued good-naturedly about the statistics of the school Daniel's team would play Friday in the state basketball tournament until Erica broke in. "Chad, I heard the odds in your favor at the mine shortened today. How come?"

Darting a sharp glance at Sabina, Chad snapped, "Where did you hear about that pool?"

"The guys were talking about it when I was out at the site, and I saw Moogie on my way home from play practice today." Her eyes were mischievous as they turned to Sabina. "Moogie said Jonas started the turnaround in the betting. You didn't scare poor dear Jonas, did you, Sabina?"

"I haven't the faintest idea what you're talking about. We got along beautifully, even though he has an unfortunate way of treating me—as if I were about eight.'' Sabina grinned at the memory of her encounter with the little man that morning.

Erica looked at her brother, who frowned and shook his head.

Chad asked tautly, ''How much time have you been spending at the site, Erica? I thought the play kept you busy after school.''

She lowered her eyes, but her voice was defiant as she answered, ''My part isn't on stage until the second act. They're working on act one this week.'' She continued defensively, ''I like being out there. The guys answer my questions and treat me as if I could do anything they can. Don't worry, Chad. Tom and Moogie keep an eye on Bobbie. He never comes near me.''

''Women have no business at the cut. Even though you're protected, there's always the danger of an accident. Sabina *has* to be there. She knows what she's doing, but as soon as she finishes the inspection, I'll keep her away from the area. I don't want to risk either of you getting injured.''

''Is *that* what Sabina's here for?'' Daniel came out of his absorption with the rapidly disappearing food on his plate. ''I thought she just sort of came down to put an okay on everything.''

Chad's chauvinism made Sabina's blood boil. She resolved to find a way to show him she was as competent as any man. Rather than cause a scene at the table, she answered Daniel's question.

''Everything has to meet state guidelines, Daniel. A

lot of people think a woman would be easy to fool. I'm not.''

''I expect the men were looking for someone a mite older and tougher on the eyes, not a little bitty thing like you,'' interjected Clara, who had been uncharacteristically quiet until now. ''Beats me how men think any woman who takes a responsible job has to be middle-aged and have a face as plain as a plate.''

Giggles immersed the twins, while Chad sighed and favored Sabina with a laughing glance. ''Now you've set Clara off on women's rights. Since the whole thing is exactly what she's believed all her life, she can't understand what all the fuss is about.'' His grin was wicked as he teased, ''Maybe you can switch her to the subject of environmentalists and whether they should be given food and shelter.''

Chapter Three

"Are you an *environmentalist?*" Erica's tone implied equal status with a child-abuser.

Since the beginning of her career, Sabina had encountered the same attitude. She was seldom given a chance to present her case in a rational manner. But now she had *two* battles to fight. Something simmered between her and the watchful man across the table, a chemical reaction which had occurred without any contact. If contact ever took place . . .

His grin was already complacent. She couldn't let that happen. Quickly scrambling her thoughts into line, she said, "Environmentalist, preservationist, conservationist . . . whatever you want to call me. I simply don't like to see acres of natural beauty ripped open, gutted, and left abused. If you saw what I've encountered out west, or even as close as Kentucky, you'd know what I mean." Still sensing hostility, she said, "In all fairness, Ohio makes a terrific effort to control that kind of thing."

"Hasn't Chad shown you . . . ?"

"All in good time, Daniel. Sabina spent today at the new site." Chad's voice cut across the boy's question, and his look held his cousin quiet. "I'm sure she

34

won't jump to any conclusions before she's seen what we do. We have to teach her that surface mining can benefit everyone.''

He wasn't sure he wanted her to stay, but he was positive he didn't want her to leave. No state inspector had the right to be so very feminine or smell so good. He could get in over his head without even trying.

He watched Sabina's spine stiffen. Then she delighted him by responding unthinkingly, ''I'm sure I'll be interested in whatever you have to teach, Chad.''

Caution flying to the wind, he seized the opening. For the first time since he'd met her, he was on familiar ground. When it came to innuendo, he was very much at home. He said softly, ''I'm counting on it.''

No one could have missed the seductive timbre of his voice. There was sudden intense interest in the cooling food on three plates.

Clara rose, ostensibly to remove the dinner plates, her eyes twinkling. ''Behave yourself now, Chad,'' she said.

Jumping to her feet, Erica said brightly, ''I have a Latin Club meeting.'' She cast a knowing glance at Sabina's tightening mouth and the stiff set of her head before adding, ''I sure hope I'm not going to miss anything good.''

As he rose, Daniel repeated soberly, ''You heard what Gran said, Chad,'' and followed his sister. His laughter punctuated the sound of their feet echoing on the hardwood floor.

Chad appeared to ignore his cousins' exit. His golden glance held hers.

He'd treated her comments and questions this morning with the respect he would give another professional. Now he was looking at her as if he were the wolf and she were Red Riding Hood. And Sabina felt like the red-caped little innocent. It was difficult to remember her job when her heart beat wildly in her throat.

This was her own fault. She'd given him the opening with her careless response, and he wasn't enough of a gentleman to let the remark slide. Chad's relatives were obviously accustomed to applauding whatever he did. Small wonder he probably thought he could walk on water.

If this small-town lothario thought he would give her a treat, Sabina decided, he was in for a surprise, even though he emanated more horsepower than she'd ever encountered.

Sabina tore her gaze free, inhaled deeply, and said, "Tell me more about small-town banking, Chad. Aren't most of the small, family-owned banks being bought out by the larger chains?"

Chad had obviously expected her to rise to his bait. Her change of subject startled him, and he answered blankly, "Yes. That is, uh, a lot of them are."

Sabina maintained a polite expression. Her change of subject worked. Forsaking his attempt at flirtation, Chad chuckled. "One up to you, Sabina," he said softly. "Actually, there are only four banks. All small, all rural, and all extremely conservative about loans but creative in their investments. We're very solid, and our customers like the local touch."

The swinging door from the kitchen flew open. "Here's dessert. Hot apple pie with cheese. Eat it while it's warm." The plates landed surely in front of each of them. "Don't pick on my guest, Chad. She's a nice girl, and she can't help what she does for a living. Remember the time the revenuers came to visit Uncle Tim Hawkins. He was polite even while they smashed his still. You can learn from his good manners."

"Sabina doesn't need your protection, Aunt Clara. The lady can take care of herself."

Clara filled a cup from the carafe she'd set on the table. "I'm glad to hear that, 'cause I have to get to circle before they give me a committee. Happens every time I miss."

Sabina lowered her gaze to her plate and said demurely, "I don't think Chad has done a thing to change my first impression, Mrs. Kincaid."

"He's a good boy, and he works hard. Goin' away to school gave him some notions, so every once in a while I have to remind him how to behave, but I trust him." She bustled out the door.

Chad's amused glance followed her, then swung to meet Sabina's. "Looks like I'll have to work to restore my standing." He burst out laughing at the beating his image had just taken.

Relieved that the tension had broken, Sabina joined him.

"We'll clear the table when we get back, Chad. You and Sabina can just go on giggling and whatever," Erica's voice broke in from the archway.

Chad checked his mirth long enough to gasp, "Go."

Sabina wondered how he dealt with having a Greek chorus bring him up short when he was trying to be macho. Her own family never teased each other. They were serious about privacy, and this open, rather rude humor was new to her. John had been serious too, she recalled, realizing it had been months since she'd given her ex-fiancé a thought.

The startled expression on her face caught Chad's attention. "You look as if you just stepped through the looking glass."

Faced with his steady regard, she settled for a half truth. "Nothing, really. I was just feeling envious because you're all so comfortable with each other. You really don't mind that they tease you in front of a complete stranger."

"In my family, you take care of yourself or you're dead. Now, if *you* should take it into your head to insult me, you'd find yourself standing very much on your own. We don't allow outsiders the same freedom."

"That's what I thought." She watched the tiny pinpoints of light dancing in his eyes; there was a fine tension in the strong jut of his jaw. He could pounce with little warning. Sabina rose and yawned widely. "I hate to leave such fascinating company, but I really must call it a day. I have to transfer all my notes to forms yet, so if you'll excuse me . . ."

"Coward," he murmured as he stood and drifted halfway around the table with the effortless economy of movement she'd been so aware of during their morning inspection at the site.

Her voice sounded thin even to her own ears. "I've no idea what you're talking about. I have a job to do, and I need my rest to do it properly." Averting her eyes, she searched the paneling with fumbling fingers for the door to her suite.

Without appearing to move, Chad was ahead of her, holding open the panel. To enter, she had to pass within inches of him, through a danger zone of singing vitality. Sabina froze in place, unable to move within the perimeter of his aura.

"You're afraid I'll touch you. You should be." The gaze locked on hers was a blaze of deep amber; the caressing voice would have tempted Mother Teresa.

Although a spiral of pure anticipation curled deep within her, she said evasively, "I'll see you tomorrow at your office."

His eyes held her gaze briefly, then he smiled. "I'll pick you up. There are several places I want to show you in the afternoon." He moved closer. "Remember, I have to educate you . . . about creative reclamation."

"I'm sure there's little you can show me I don't already know." She felt as if she weren't getting enough air.

His fingers smoothed her hair behind her ear, the movement intentionally provocative. As his hand traveled a knowing path over the shining strands, each individual hair clung to his skin. She felt his warm breath pulse against her forehead as he whispered, "We'll just have to find out, won't we?"

Sabina panicked and ran.

Chad watched her desperate disappearance. It was just as well. In another minute he might have made an idiot of himself. The lady from the state looked like a wide-eyed innocent, but underneath he sensed intelligence, cleverness, and stubbornness. She didn't back off. Maybe she possessed as much arrogance as he did.

The scent of jasmine lingered in his nostrils. He would enjoy bringing each nugget of her personality to the surface. The thought amused him. After all, he was a miner, wasn't he?

The next morning, Sabina stood in the shower longer than usual. After claiming exhaustion, she had tossed and turned throughout the night. The scene at her door last night had unnerved her, yet she found she could barely wait to engage the enemy again. She turned off the taps.

The tempting aromas of coffee and frying ham permeating the air made her hurry, and she dressed quickly and searched out the homey kitchen. Crisp, no-nonsense yellow-and-white checked curtains covering a row of tall windows appeared to capture and magnify the sun pouring through them.

"You're just in time, Sabina. Erica, go finish dryin' your hair. You'll catch your death if you go out in the cold with a damp head." Clara rested her hands on apron-covered hips and eyed Sabina's Icelandic wool sweater and twill slacks with approval. "Your boots are all clean. I put them next to the register so's you'll start off warm. How do you like your eggs?"

Sabina protested, "Mrs. Kincaid, you didn't have to do that."

"Don't thank her. You haven't seen her bill yet," Erica threw over her shoulder as she left.

Ignoring the saucy interruption, Clara demanded, "About those eggs . . ."

Chastened, Sabina took the seat Erica had vacated. "Scrambled, please. If it isn't too much trouble."

Chad's voice, low and teasing, reached her ear. "Actually, if she hadn't taken a liking to you, your boots could have rotted on the back step."

"I heard that, Chad Peters. You just eat your flap-jacks and tend your own business." Clara's voice held authority.

Sabina tilted a grumpy look in Chad's direction. "You're certainly cheerful this morning." She found mornings impossible until she had had at least two cups of coffee.

As if guessing her problem, Chad moved a glass and a pitcher of orange juice in front of her before filling a blue and white mug with steaming coffee. "Here. Drink up and join the living."

Without turning, Clara commented, "He always was one for wakin' up on both feet. It's never seemed natural for someone to smile that much before break-fast. I wouldn't have let him in the door this morning if he hadn't insisted he'd come to pick you up."

"Now, Aunt Clara, I'm just being cooperative. You don't want her to make a bad report on Calico, do you?"

After sipping her coffee, Sabina said dryly, "I think

it's more a case for the courts, Mrs. Kincaid. My department doesn't deal in rehabilitation.''

Chad poured golden honey over his pancakes and smiled sunnily. ''Some of us are even grumpy at lunch.'' His look challenged her to remember her testiness of the day before.

She ignored him while she inspected the plate of ham and eggs Clara had deposited in front of her, hoping the aroma of the food would overpower the scent of soap, fresh air, and masculinity which seemed to surround her. Eating breakfast next to so much vitality stimulated more than her appetite for food.

Clara brought her own brimming plate to the table. ''Don't know what's gotten into Daniel lately. He's polite and helpful, but he's been awful quiet lately. You best have a talk with him, Chad.''

''He's a senior, Aunt Clara. He has a lot on his mind . . . classes, that girlfriend, and the state basketball tournament. I could use his help at the mine, but there's no point in pressuring him. Give him some space.''

''Somethin's eatin' at him, but I can't put a finger on it.'' Clara cut a piece of thick pink ham. ''All I say is, he might talk to you before he will me. If it's women, you'd be the one to know.'' She placed the meat in her mouth and chewed thoughtfully.

Sabina struggled to swallow her laughter, choked, then cleared her throat instead.

Clara's observations about his private life had amused Chad for years. Today the public reference irritated him. Reports of his personal activities had always circulated through the small community, mostly because no one had anything else to talk about. Actually, he was flattered, because no human could keep up such a pace. Not while he managed two demanding businesses.

Seeing the curiosity in the cobalt blue eyes watching him, he realized he had been judged and found guilty. "I imagine you can tell him anything he really needs to know, Aunt Clara."

He watched Sabina seek refuge in the food in front of her. He knew his sudden shifts in mood confused her, but they were new to him, too. He wondered what was causing the solemn expression on her face.

The only man Sabina had ever spent much time with was her ex-fiancé, and they'd both been so zealous in their defense of the environment that laughter and teasing had never been part of their courtship. After their breakup, she'd felt both relief and guilt. Now only the relief remained. She dragged herself back to the present and looked up to see laughter lurking in her hostess's merry brown eyes as she said, "Maybe I'd best send Daniel 'round to Jonas with his questions."

Chad and his aunt grinned at the idea, and Sabina felt curiously left out. She finished her meal in silence, while her breakfast partners discussed local happenings. She filed one statement away for future consideration, and said, "We'd better get started, Chad. I have a lot of ground to cover, and time is short." Sabina stood decisively before adding, "Everything was delicious, Mrs. Kincaid. I'm glad I won't be here long. I'd have to let out all my clothes.''

Chad watched her slender back disappear through the swinging door, admiring the trim fit of the wool slacks swinging jauntily from her hips. ''We couldn't have that, could we, Aunt Clara?''

''That's a nice young woman, Chad. Don't you go getting her riled. I called Moogie this morning myself and put my money on her. He said the odds were even.''

He grinned. ''I'm crushed. First money said I'd send her back to Columbus with a bug in her ear. Now my own family expects me to be the loser. Such loyalty!''

''I talked to Jonas last night. He says she knows as much as you do.''

''She may know theory, but she hasn't figured out how to apply it creatively. Given time, I bet I could make a convert of her.'' Lazy speculation that had nothing to do with mining drifted through his mind. His eyes narrowed.

Clara considered his expression warily. ''Now, Chad, you behave yourself.''

The ride in the frigid Jeep didn't reassure Sabina. Chad had reverted to brooding silence, broken only by his comment as the ever-present Labrador nuzzled her cheek from behind the seat. ''He has a thing for women's makeup. He licks it off.''

''He's welcome to any he can find.'' Sabina answered tartly. She wore only enough makeup to maintain her self-confidence. Her job was to ensure proper practices—not to win beauty contests.

The spiraling tension she felt was tripled in the confines of the Jeep; she furtively inhaled the wonderful aroma of clean, early-morning male. Stealing a glance from beneath her lashes, she surveyed the sharp, shaven line of his jaw, the slightly thickened bridge of his otherwise straight nose. She wondered how he had broken it, visualizing athletic contests—or even a brawl with one of his employees.

The scrap of Clara's breakfast conversation surfaced in her thoughts. "What did your aunt mean about buyers calling?"

His eyes steady on the highway, Chad answered, "Oil companies and foreign investors have discovered small mining companies. Actually, they want the mineral rights we've contracted more than the companies themselves."

"But why?"

"Coal is plentiful here, but most of it is high-sulfur. The market has dwindled because of clean air regulations. Some of the operators are glad to sell cheap to get out from under." He sounded uneasy, as if the subject were distasteful to him.

A penny dropped in Sabina's mind. "But technology is on the brink of solving the sulfur problem. When that happens . . ."

"Whoever owns the rights will control the energy the coal represents," he finished, pleased by her quick understanding.

"Are you going to sell Calico?"

Chad asked himself the same question with annoying regularity. Hearing it from Sabina's lips made him feel selfish and disloyal—traits he despised. His curt answer gave nothing away. ''Not this week.''

Chad parked in front of the concrete block building, swinging fluidly to the asphalt before the engine died. In a display of misplaced loyalty, Sock exited on Sabina's side of the mud-splattered vehicle, causing Chad to mumble beneath his breath about the fickleness of man's closest companions.

Sabina followed Chad to the privacy of his office, once again confused. Where was the man who'd greeted her so cheerfully at breakfast? His silence seemed to bounce off the walls. The welcome aroma of freshly made coffee filled the air. Sabina had a feeling she would need it.

Sun filtered through the miniblinds to highlight the polished surface of the oak desk, skitter over cranberry carpet, and come up short at the base of a pine-paneled wall. The room was clean and neat—a vast improvement over most mining company offices she'd visited. There wasn't even a girlie calendar or a bulletin board of yellowed ''good ol' boy'' cartoons. She decided Chad's banker's orderliness must carry over into his second job.

The walls were hung with large, framed, color photographs of scenery—not calendar art, but beautifully matted scenes of flower-strewn meadows and stands of young trees.

''What stunning pictures!'' she exclaimed, pausing in front of a particularly appealing shot of a well-designed housing development. A sweeping hillside of pines rose behind it.

Chad's smile was triumphant. "Reclaimed land, Sabina. Each of those once looked just like the ugly mess you saw yesterday. The family's been doing this the right way for years. Since before there were strict rules." He opened a large metal cabinet behind the desk. "Now we can get down to business."

Sabina viewed with dismay the stack of neatly labeled manila folders, the photo albums, and the tidy rolls of topical maps. "Surely it won't be necessary to go through *all* of that."

"You're the one who wants to check every step. By the time we're finished, you'll know exactly what that land looked like before and what it will look like when we finish—not to mention how we're going to do it. And we'll go over the last two sites the same way." He placed several folders and an album on the desk.

His voice took on a different timbre, his eyes darkened, and he moved toward her. "Just you and me, huddled over all this paperwork. But first let's get this out of the way." He spoke casually, as if in afterthought.

She felt the warmth of his fingers as he took hold of her arms, and stiffened as he turned her toward him. "Ever since you popped up at the site, I've wondered what you taste like. I can't wait any longer."

Sabina froze in place, mesmerized by the golden glow of his eyes, incapable of protesting. She breathed shallowly.

His eyes darkened. "I was afraid of this," he murmured, as he lowered his head.

Sabina responded to his touch by instinct. She felt as if her soul were being dredged up and opened for his inspection; she couldn't back away. Even if she had wanted to.

The kiss ended as abruptly as it had begun. The challenging light in Chad's clear eyes told her this was only the beginning.

"Now we can get to work. Coffee?"

Anger at his arrogance brought heat to Sabina's cheeks. What had she been thinking to allow him to take control like that? She gathered assurance around her like a wrinkled cape and managed to meet his eyes without wavering. "Yes, thank you. Just as it comes from the pot. I hope you have a lot. We have a long day ahead of us."

Chad filled a lipstick-red mug and extended it. She had no recourse but to brush her fingers against the warmth of his as she took it. She accepted the risk.

Chapter Four

Sabina drew her pen from her briefcase. "Your permits first, Chad." She paused to sip the steaming coffee. "Let's start on the same page."

Silently battling a quickened pulse which astounded him, Chad furnished the originals. The slight tremor of her hands gave him some satisfaction. It was only fair that she be as shaken as he.

They worked for the next hour, limiting conversation to the necessary, while the kiss simmered between them like a campfire.

Chad watched the play of expressions on her face, surprised by the warmth beneath his breastbone. Never before had such trivial details about a woman triggered this rush of tenderness. Even at her most suspicious and professional, he found Sabina enchanting. The realization made him smile.

"Is something funny, Chad? Everything looks perfect so far, but if you continue to smile so secretively, I'll think you're trying to put something over on me."

All the material he'd furnished was textbook-perfect. Her natural caution pleased him.

"A private joke, Sabina. One on me," he added truthfully.

When the phone rang, she continued her perusal of the papers on the desk, politely ignoring Chad's conversation. *The man's going to drive me crazy with that half smile,* she told herself.

"Another call from the bank," he apologized. It was the third thus far. "Can we reschedule some of this? I have to be there this afternoon, and I want to show you some reclaimed sites before lunch."

His distracted expression softened Sabina's heart. In a complete reversal of her unsympathetic attitude the day before, she accommodated herself to his problem without hesitation. "I can finish this tomorrow. Let me take those photo albums and the topical maps. I'll look them over this evening."

Coming much too close for her comfort, Chad rested one warm hand on her forehead. "No fever. Did I hear you correctly? Is this the same woman who tried to tear me apart yesterday because I didn't salute when she spoke?"

Sabina slapped his hand away. She wanted him to kiss her again; the realization stunned her. "If you'd been honest at the beginning, I would have been more understanding. Let's not waste any more time."

The fine lines around his eyes crinkled as he leered melodramatically. "Does my work ethic turn you on?"

Sabina wanted desperately to respond in kind. She didn't dare, not with the scented breeze coming in the window announcing the miracle of a false spring. The combination could be fatal.

As if agreeing with her assessment, Chad said, "I'll

bring the albums. We can look at them over lunch.''
He tucked them under one arm, opened the door, and
guided her through.

The desk in the small lobby was no longer unoc-
cupied. A thirtyish woman hunched over the keyboard.
Her head lifted slowly, adoration in the look she gave
Chad. "Chad! I thought you'd be here all morning."

He rested the books on the desk and pulled Sabina's
jacket from the old-fashioned rack in the corner.
"They need me at the bank, Edna, and Ms. Hanlon
and I have to visit some sites. Will you be all right
alone here?"

The woman's smile, slow in coming, was blinding.
"I'll be fine, Chad. Dad's coming for me at one
o'clock."

Her eyes traveled curiously to Sabina, and Chad in-
troduced her. Sabina realized the girl's adoration now
included her, and extended a warm greeting as she
buttoned her coat.

"You won't need your scarf or your hood, Ms.
Hanlon. It was real pleasant when I came in." Edna
enunciated each word with great care.

Sabina thanked her, then preceded Chad through the
door. He boosted her into the Jeep, placed the albums
on her lap, and fastened her seat belt before disappearing around the rear of the vehicle. He was in the
driver's seat by the time she caught her breath. Sock
scrambled in behind them.

He smiled at her. "Thank you for being sweet to
Edna. She's a sort of cousin. She's educable, and has
a knack for computer entries, once she knows what's

required. She works here four hours a day. It's important for her to feel she's contributing . . . and she is.''

Sabina visualized Chad as the head of a clan. All problems seemed to lead to his door.

She recalled his lighthearted teasing last evening—and the matter-of-fact way he'd approached kissing her this morning. A kiss which had been rather more than matter-of-fact.

"How did you break your nose?" she asked, desperate to break the silence.

The Jeep swung around a corner and settled back into its normal stiff ride. He swiveled, treating her to a wicked grin. "Nothing very romantic. I walked into the edge of the dining room table when I was five. My mother said it would be a permanent reminder to me to watch where I was going." He laughed ruefully.

"Sounds as if you didn't get much sympathy."

"She was hugging me when she said it." They bumped along a narrow mining road which branched off the highway. The clear air was almost addictive.

Sabina unbuttoned the top button of her coat, then stuffed her woolen gloves into her pocket. She wanted to get out of the Jeep and revel in the scented breeze. As if in response to her unspoken wish, they plunged to a stop.

"This is a good place to start," Chad threw over his shoulder as he climbed out.

Sabina joined him. Acres of land spread before her, the earth slick and damp beneath a sparse cover of dead grasses. The landscape was a blur of subtle contours sloping to the left toward a meandering creek.

"Was that the stream you diverted?" She visualized the paperwork; the diversion had been creative, avoiding disturbance of the water table during the operation.

His expression patient and solemn, Chad responded, "Yes, ma'am. And now the creek's back where it was before we began."

Sabina swallowed the temptation to stick out her tongue at him. "What kinds of trees are those?" She pointed right, where a slope of seedlings climbed toward a heavily wooded area.

"Pine, oak, walnut, maple, ash, spruce, locust, lots of dogwood . . . I'm partial to dogwood in the spring . . . plus anything else that will grow here." Enthusiasm lit his voice. "Follow me to the creek so you can see how it's coming along."

Wordlessly, Sabina followed his effortless stride across the field. He seemed to know instinctively where the footing was solid; only once did mud suck at her boot. Sock ranged far to their left, spraying muddy water as he threw himself through flat, shallow puddles of melting snow.

The swollen creek flowed briskly between its banks. She knew that when the earth bloomed the site would be beautiful.

It was difficult to superimpose this over the horrors she'd seen elsewhere. Chad seemed a part of the scene in front of her. His fluid grace drew her like a pied piper. She'd been so entranced by his movements and the way the sun burrowed into his tawny hair that she'd nearly forgotten why they were there.

"When Zack and I were kids, we always went to the woods in the early spring. When we returned home soaking wet, Zack would say I'd fallen in and he'd leaped in to save me. He was five years older than I." Chad's voice broke, then steadied. "I think I was twenty before my mother admitted she'd used the same lie when she was a kid. Some things never change."

With a gesture toward raw sections of the creek bed, she answered sadly, "This has."

"Give it a few more years. You'll never know anything disturbed it." Chad's words were clipped; his gaze challenged her. "If you don't believe me, come back and see."

Her narrowed eyes questioned his claim; her voice was as firm as her look. "I just might do that."

"I like you, Sabina Hanlon. I really do. You'd spit in my eye if you thought I deserved it." He planted a smacking kiss on her forehead, whirled, and led the way back toward the Jeep.

She stomped behind him, his impulsive words lingering in her ears. The clean smell of thawing earth, the plaintive calls of mourning doves, the gusting wind—all went unnoticed. Sabina was mad.

As they reached the Jeep, she grabbed his arm. He offered no resistance. "Do you kiss all the deputy inspectors who come your way?"

Chad was exhilarated. The sights, sounds, and smells of spring affected him like wine. Was it because she said she might return? Ridiculous. If he wanted her back, she'd come. Or would she? He'd realized from the start that Sabina Hanlon wouldn't leap at anyone's bidding—unless she wanted to. The thought pleased him more than it frustrated him. "I never saw one as pretty as you before." He looked down at her hand clutching his upper arm and asked lightly, "Are you going to flip me over your shoulder now?"

"Do you think I can't?"

He looked deeply into her eyes. They were wide and dark, and her breathing was shallow. It was gratifying to discover that this unorthodox conversation effected her as much as it did him. "I warn you, I've kept some rough company. It would go against the grain to use some of my tricks on a woman."

"I knew you were a wimp. With surprise on my side, I bet I could take you down," she challenged.

"You want to make book?"

"You mean like the betting at the mine site?"

He reached out to tousle her hair as he'd been wanting to all morning. The soft, belled cut fell back automatically into its tidy curve. "Who taught you to defend yourself?"

"One of my college instructors. He said I might come across a smart-mouthed miner and need to put him in his place. He didn't mention bankers."

"He should have. Are you hungry?"

"I'm starved," Sabina answered honestly, hoping her dizziness was simple hunger.

"We can kill two birds with one stone." He latched

the door behind her, then swung into the driver's seat. "We'll eat in an area that was mined eleven years ago." He lifted two fingers to his lips and whistled. Moments later Sock appeared, mud caking his sleek body. Chad fished a tattered bath towel from the back of the jeep to remove the worst before allowing the dog to clamber behind the seat, then started the Jeep.

Sabina was lost. The winding trails they followed couldn't be on any map, and she jounced from left to right, struggling to keep hold of the bulky photo albums. "Where are we going?" she shouted above the motor's roar as they swept up a rutted track that looked as if it had been abandoned sometime during Teddy Roosevelt's administration.

"You'll see," he replied, concentrating on controlling the Jeep. "This is a shortcut. Only the natives know it."

They topped a small rise, the woods still thick around them. The muddy vehicle took one last headlong swoop and came to a stop. The track ended abruptly behind an A-frame nestled on a plateau. The mature trees which had surrounded them had vanished, giving way to growth perhaps half as high as the earlier forest. The building merged into the landscape.

"Where are we?"

"At my house." Pride of possession radiated in his voice.

"I thought we were coming to see another reclaimed site."

"You're standing on one. Zack mined and reclaimed this whole section." The beauty of the coun-

tryside around him stood for an accomplishment—
something tangible by which to remember his cousin.
"After the accident, I bought fifty acres to keep as a
memory. Isn't it beautiful?"

Through the half-grown trees, Sabina saw fast-
moving water. Sunlight danced across its surface. "I
suppose that creek was also put back in its original
course?" She couldn't help injecting skepticism, even
though she was sure of the answer.

"Of course. These streams all drain toward the
Muskingum River, so we take good care of them. Can
you imagine what the Y-Bridge in Zanesville would
look like without any water beneath it? The tourists
wouldn't come and take pictures."

"Everyone talks about that bridge as if it were one
of the seven wonders, but I haven't figured out the
necessity." This was a Chad she hadn't yet seen. Instead of treating her as a nosy intruder in the close-
knit fraternity of the area, he was sharing his affection
for the land and its history.

"A tributary comes in at the natural crossing, and
the original bridge connected three different settle-
ments. Now they're one town. Pilots flying cross-
country in the early days used the Y-Bridge to get their
bearings. The old National Road went due west from
the bridge, and the planes followed it."

All of a sudden, Chad realized he sounded like an
agent for the local tourist bureau, but he shrugged and
went on. "I have an article about it inside. I'll make
you a copy."

Sabina watched the fast-moving creek, visualizing

the flowing water joining other tributaries and flowing under the legendary bridge. "Where does the Muskingum go?"

"To the Ohio, then into the Mississippi, and on to the Gulf of Mexico. When I was a kid, I resented the water I was watching doing all that traveling without me. Zack and I thought we pretty much owned all the creeks around here."

"I'll bet the two of you thought you owned just about everything in sight," Sabina teased.

Chad grinned sheepishly. "Aunt Clara said we were 'big feelin', but she never had any trouble jerking us into line."

An ominous rumble from her midsection reminded Sabina of her hunger. She shifted the albums to one arm and stepped out of the Jeep. "We'd better find lunch before I get cranky." As she spoke, the impact of where they were hit her. She stopped in mid movement.

His clear, flexible voice, capable of so many different levels of warmth, came from disturbingly close.

" 'Come into my parlor,' said the villain."

She jumped, clutching the books in front of her as if for protection. "Why did you sneak up on me?"

"I'm testing your defenses. Here, give me those. This path gets slippery." He led the way surefootedly. "We'll make subs, and you can look at the albums while you eat."

Sabina breathed an inward sigh of relief. The menu hardly sounded like an invitation to seduction. Perhaps the only real danger from Chad Peters existed in her own fevered imagination.

"No, Sock. You can't come in till you've had a bath." Chad held the door for her as the dog disappeared around the corner of the house. "The garage and my recreation room are down here. Give me your coat."

Sunlight and the sheen of highly polished natural woods greeted her as she climbed the last tread. The whole room was open, save for the wall behind a vast central fireplace, which created the illusion of a separate kitchen. Broad windows gave on the stark winter landscape around them. Sabina was enchanted.

"Do the deer come close?" she asked as she gravitated toward the expansive view. Comfortable upholstered chairs and sofas were arranged near the windows, and others were grouped in front of the fireplace. Light, natural wood paneling matched the hardwood floors gleaming between jewel-toned area rugs.

"They like to look in at me. I keep a salt lick out for them. Do you want to see the view from the deck upstairs before lunch?"

At her suspicious look, he held up two fingers. "Scout's honor. You'll love the view. Period."

Sabina approached the stairway. "Must I remind you I work for the State of Ohio? We aren't allowed to flirt on the job."

"Does that mean you flirt after working hours?"

Sabina ignored him. At the landing, Chad drew her through a door at the end of the hall, then stood back to await her reaction.

"Skylights!" Her head tilted, she looked up at the rectangles of sunlight on each side of the roofline. Sunlight flowed through them and met in the center of the room, creating a suspended diamond of gold. More light flooded in through the sliding glass door.

Chad watched her blissful expression, pleased by her reaction. "You like my hideaway?"

"I love it." Since her broken engagement, she'd pushed romance from her life, applying her energies to her work. Now, with Chad so near, and with her thoughts skittering in all directions, she felt inept.

"Come out on the deck." Chad crossed to the sliding glass door, beckoning to her to join him. The whole countryside lay before their eyes.

"The earth's awakening," she breathed, leaning on the railing. "Everything's been hibernating, and a few more days of this will bring a miracle."

"The snowdrops are out already. Around here we always say there will be at least six inches of snow before anything else can bloom." The buoyant weather tested his restraint. She was wary, making him move with the caution he used with the wild creatures who came to inspect his wooded hideaway.

He felt Sabina move away slightly. Her face was flushed, as if she were making conversation to fill the silence.

"Having your hot tub up here is a real luxury. You can . . ." Her words trickled to silence.

Chad bit his lip to keep from laughing at her confusion. "It's a good way to relax after a long day."

He turned from her. "Much as I hate to say this, we have to hurry along and eat lunch, or I'll be late."

His abrupt change of subject renewed Sabina's ability to breathe. Her relief almost tangible, she followed him through the light-filled room and down the stairs.

Chad was already pulling paper-wrapped packages from the refrigerator. He opened a bakery bag containing fresh, fragrant buns and added them to the array of cheeses and meats on the counter.

"Nothing elegant, but it should do the trick," he said as he pulled out a coffee filter. "Coffee or tea?"

"Milk, if you have it," she replied, her hands busy layering salami and ham with cheeses.

He stuffed the filter back in the box and pulled two tumblers from the cupboard. By the time the glasses were in place on the maple table in front of the picture window, she was sliding into her chair. "You don't waste any time when you're hungry, do you?" he joked.

"I'm starved. Where did you put those albums?"

Wordlessly, he retrieved them from the couch, passed them to her, and made his own sandwich.

They ate in a silence broken only by Sabina's tiny sounds of approval. Finally, he asked, "Is it the food or the photographs causing those little punctuation marks you're making? You sound like Victor Borge."

She swallowed, her eyes still on the pages in front of her, before answering, "Both."

Chad concentrated on his sandwich. He'd known the pictures would be the clincher. Her report should keep them off his back for a long time. Then he realized he didn't give a hoot about the state's reaction. He wanted to impress Sabina.

"My apologies, Chad. Until I saw these, I hadn't realized you were a romantic."

Her words startled him. "A romantic?"

"I didn't believe you when you said Calico left things more beautiful than before you started. Now I do. These photos . . . and what I see outside your windows, have convinced me."

"Yesterday you accused me of playing God when I said Calico put the land back together so it was more beautiful than before. Either I'm a romantic or I have a Napoleon complex. Which one?"

An apology for that particular accusation was on the tip of her tongue, but Sabina couldn't force out the words. "It's hard enough for me to tell you I like your reclamation. I still hate surface mining."

"And that makes me a romantic?"

"I don't trust miners as a whole. Many seem to say one thing, then do another." She would compliment his work, but she refused to commit herself any further. His ego didn't need stroking. "At least you're honest."

As if reading her mind, Chad met her gaze with a look as candid as her own. "I do what I do because I have to. But thanks for the kind words. I know they cost you."

"You bet they did!" She burst into laughter and made a face at him, unconsciously tempting his self-control. "What I can't understand is why you'd consider selling Calico."

"I didn't say I would."

"But you've thought about it."

He pushed back his chair abruptly. "Let's get a move on. I'll drop you off at the mine site so Jonas can finish showing you what we do to control and neutralize runoff."

"Sorry I touched a sore spot. It's none of my business."

"You're right about that, anyway."

Grateful for anything that would put her back on her own turf, Sabina hurriedly returned the food to the refrigerator.

Twenty minutes later, she swung down from the Jeep, coaxing a confused Sock to follow her. "Come on, Sock. This is where all the fun is. You might get your nose caught in a ledger if you stay with him."

"With a mouth like that, I'm surprised they let you run around loose without a keeper, Ms. Deputy Inspector."

Chapter Five

The front-end loader's heavy engine roared, filling the air with sound as Chad ran toward the vast cut in the earth, but he was accustomed to the roar. What he wasn't accustomed to was seeing the entire crew standing at the edge.

"Who's operating that thing?" he shouted. Several options occurred to him, and he didn't care for any of them.

The group dissolved, leaving a sheepish-looking Jonas a target for his wrath. As the little man searched for words, Chad looked down at the two safety-helmeted heads in the cab. Blond hair hung below the hat of the figure at the controls. "Jonas, you idiot!" Fear froze him in his tracks.

"Keep your shirt on, Chad. It's all . . ." Jonas's words trailed off as the machine stopped. Silence engulfed them.

Tight-lipped, Chad watched the two figures climb down, glance upward, and head for the earthen ramp. Jonas stood his ground, shuffling his feet and looking as if he wished aliens would whisk him away in a spaceship.

He saw Sabina put a hand on Erica's arm and squeeze past her to be first to reach the top.

Mud splattered the cuffs of Sabina's trim slacks. Her down jacket hung open. She'd pulled off her yellow hat, and the brisk breeze lifted her hair. More mud graced her right cheek. She met his gaze calmly as he approached. "Chad, you shouldn't be upset with Erica."

In spite of his fury, he appreciated her directness. "Why limit me? I'm furious with Erica, with Jonas, with that whole crew of careless idiots who work with him, and last but not least, dear madam inspector, with you!"

If Chad had shouted, Sabina could have responded in kind. His menacing purr sent an unpleasant chill up her spine. When she opened her mouth to speak, Chad raised his hand to stop her and turned on Jonas. His language was nothing Sabina hadn't heard before, but the silky voice made the words more effective. Under different circumstances, she would have admired his creativity in connecting the familiar invectives.

Jonas stood his ground beneath the barrage of abuse. Finally he said soothingly, "Chad, I'm sorry your pa ain't here to hear you. You'd do him proud."

Chad's tirade stopped in mid sentence. "You old coot. Don't pull that 'family retainer' routine on me. What possessed you to let Erica operate that loader? Don't we have an ironclad rule that novices have to be accompanied by someone who's checked out on the equipment? What if Miss Hanlon had been injured?''

''Guess you know why I didn't tell you Erica's bin learnin'. Besides, Miss Hanlon's licensed for everything we got.''

Sabina extended a clear plastic pouch of papers.

Chad ignored her. His frown deepened. ''Nobody here is listening to me. I don't care if Sabina is licensed to fly the Concorde. She doesn't belong in our equipment. As for teaching an eighteen-year-old girl to operate a loader . . .''

Each word, clipped and cold, chilled Sabina more than the rapidly falling temperature.

''Chad, that's not fair. I have every right. You *made* Daniel learn.'' Tears thickened Erica's voice.

His cousin's anguish caught at Chad's heart. When Zack and Marie died, he'd promised himself the twins would never be hurt again. He wanted to comfort her, but he was still frightened. ''You know how I feel about you being out here. You could get hurt, and there's always the risk one of the men will step out of line. I don't want to have to fire anyone. These people need their jobs to feed their families.''

''No one would touch Erica, Chad. And every one of 'em would die before they'd let someone else,'' Jonas broke in.

Sabina swallowed her sympathy. Granted, Chad was being remarkably obtuse and stubborn, but she understood the awesome responsibility he felt toward the twins. If only he weren't so uncompromising—and so chauvinistic.

Her involvement in the tense little scene was so complete that she ignored the pressure at the back of her knees. A moment later she found herself sprawled on the ground, with Sock nosing her face and licking her cheeks.

"Get away, Sock. I'm mud all the way up to my ears." Laughter shook Sabina's voice as she reached to scratch his chin.

His face devoid of expression, Chad held out his hand.

Sabina waved him away, displaying her muddy palm for his inspection. "I can manage." Turning sideways, she levered herself erect, her boots sliding on the slick surface.

"I guess it's too late to apologize," Chad said. "It's bad enough you had to witness my temper tantrum. Now you know the dog doesn't have any manners either."

"On the contrary. *He* said he was sorry when he licked my face," she shot back. "At least he didn't swear at me."

"I didn't swear at *you*."

"No, but you would have if you'd dared. I never knew I exercised so much power until now."

As if Erica and Jonas had disappeared, he said softly, "I don't think you've even begun to realize your power."

Sabina returned his blazing look, unable to speak around the tightness in her throat.

* * *

Their audience and surroundings came back to Chad with a rush. Erica eyed him with avid curiosity, and Jonas grinned from ear to ear. Chad wondered how long it would take the old man to increase his bet on the lady inspector. "You'd better get back and clean up, Sabina. Take Erica with you in the Jeep. Jonas will bring me in."

Erica's mouth opened as if she were about to speak. At Sabina's warning look, she shrugged her shoulders and turned toward the parking area. Sabina followed her.

The door of the Jeep hung open, the keys dangling from the ignition, mute evidence of Chad's panic. Erica pulled a tattered blanket from the back and spread it over the driver's seat. "I guess I'm not even allowed to drive this thing. You can sit on Sock's blanket, although it would serve Chad right if you got the seat good and muddy."

Sabina wiped her hands on the edge of the blanket, then started the engine. She backed with a competent flip of her wrist. "You don't really want to get even with Chad. He reacted that way because he loves you very much."

Erica's face crumpled. Tears trembled on her lashes. "Oh, Sabina, I don't know how we'd have survived without Chad. He's done so much for us. I never meant to sound as if I hated him. Honest. If he weren't my cousin I'd have such a crush on him I couldn't see straight. I'd do anything for him, Sabina."

She reached up to wipe the moisture from her eyes. "I can talk to Chad about absolutely anything but how much I want to work at the mine sites. I love being outdoors. The machinery turns me on . . . even the mud. Not very feminine, huh?''

Her lips curving in a wry smile, Sabina risked taking her attention from the rugged track. "Does that have a gender?" She looked back at the road in time to avoid a deep rut. "Those big machines do a number on me, too. Show me a tire that's taller than I am, and I'm in heaven."

She could have cut her tongue out. This wasn't her family, which never had emotional scenes. As Sabina's mother said, "Adjusted, self-sufficient people don't put themselves in situations which would inspire someone else to such an outburst."

"Why can't Chad understand? I'm eighteen, and next year I'm going to Ohio State. That's great, but I'd rather go to the Colorado School of Mines with Daniel."

She continued, "Chad's given up so much. He stayed with us at Gran's for three years. Lots of times, I know he skipped parties and stuff so he could go to things at school."

"What are you going to major in?"

"Education," Erica responded glumly. "It's not that I don't want to teach. I'd just rather run the family business."

Sabina grinned as she swung onto the main highway. "Schools are begging for science teachers. Chad can't argue with a natural sciences major. Geology courses would help you work alongside Daniel later, or you just might find you enjoy teaching science."

She paused mischievously. "If worse came to worst, you could go back to school and be a deputy inspector for the state."

The suggestion drew a giggle from Erica, who hugged herself within her denim jacket. "Why didn't I ever think of that?" Her wide, clear gaze was almost reverent as she turned toward Sabina. "That's the most perfect idea I've ever heard!"

"Just don't tell anyone I suggested it," Sabina interrupted. "I'm already in hot water with Chad."

A smirk crossed the younger girl's face. "I wouldn't worry about that. He likes you. He's eating at our house again tonight, and he never comes two nights in a row."

"Maybe after today he'll change his mind," she answered, accelerating into the driveway.

"He'll be here," Erica told her as the Jeep plunged to a stop. "Come in through the kitchen."

"I hate to track up your aunt's floor." Sabina looked ruefully down at herself.

"Gran's used to people coming in muddy. We can leave our boots on the service porch."

Minutes later, Sabina stood helplessly as Clara and Erica stripped off her mud-caked clothing. "I'll just hang these to dry. Most of that mess will brush off," Clara said.

Sabina peeled her damp sweater up over her torso. "That mud even crawled under my coat. My dry cleaner looks on me as his retirement fund."

As her sweater and slacks joined the pile of clothing, Clara handed her a blanket. "Just put this 'round you till you get to your room.'' The older woman drew back. ''My, that must be what they call one of them teddy things. I read about 'em, but this is the first one I've seen. Look, Erica, ain't it pretty? It's a shame to wear all that lace underneath.''

''I'll drink to that.''

The three women turned toward the door where Chad stood, grinning. Clara wrapped the blanket around Sabina swiftly.

''She seems warm enough already, Clara. Her cheeks're pink,'' Jonas said cheerfully, peering around Chad's shoulder.

Erica's delighted giggle broke the ensuing silence, sending Clara into action. ''You pay no heed to them, Sabina. I don't know what they're thinkin' to let Sock do his nasty tricks on you.'' She emitted an expressive ''Hmph,'' giving Sabina a firm shove in the direction of the door. ''I don't want to hear any more fresh talk.''

As she turned away, Sabina tried not to laugh at Clara's indignation. Before she swung the door closed, she heard Clara say, ''That Mr. Merton was here today lookin' for you, Chad. He must be awful anxious.''

Dismissing the serious note in Clara's voice, Sabina threw off the blanket and looked down. The lace top of her teddy didn't leave much to the imagination. Chad's interest had been obvious.

Sabina ordered herself to remember why she was here. It didn't matter that the inspection had turned out to be merely a formality. Chad did everything right.

His care of his cousin's family, or for any other shirt-tail relation, was admirable.

But the man had no business being quite so dictatorial, or so attractive. Unnerved, Sabina rushed through her shower and slipped into her pleated skirt and silk print blouse.

The table was set when she emerged. Delicious aromas drew her to the kitchen. As she reached for the door, it swung toward her and Erica burst through. "Good. I need your help," the girl whispered, drawing her into the cozy den. Opening the window seat, she pointed to a large envelope protruding from between two game boxes. "I have to go to play practice, but Daniel simply *has* to see that as soon as he gets home. I snatched it from the rest of the mail. *Don't* let Chad know anything's come for Daniel. Please help us, Sabina. This is the most important thing in Daniel's life, and Chad *can't* know about it yet."

The entreaty in her eyes completed the work the pleading speech had begun. Sabina agreed, wishing she'd never encountered this endearing family.

Erica's strong young arms enveloped her in a hearty squeeze. "I'll owe you forever."

As quickly as she'd been dragged into the conspiracy, Sabina found herself alone. Her curiosity aroused, she raised the lid to read the return address, then stepped back from the window seat when she heard Chad's voice in the hall. "It's none of my business," she lectured herself. "I don't want to be in the middle of this. The less I know, the better off I'll be."

That resolution made, she crossed the hall to the

dining room, where Chad and Jonas were about to sit down. "Glad to see you found something to wear, Sabina," Chad teased. "Although you could have kept the blanket on . . . it's just family."

The door swung wide as Clara entered, carrying a large platter of barbecued ribs. "That's enough of that, Chad. It's downright embarrassin' to think I might have to call your mother to tell her how ramshackle your manners are."

Chad didn't seem intimidated. "Calling Arizona's long distance, Aunt Clara. Remember how that runs up the phone bill? You should at least wait until the weekend to save money."

"Yer always complainin' about your bill, Clara. A call just to tell her somethin' she already knows don't make sense," Jonas contributed.

Clara turned on the little man. "I'll thank you t' keep out of family business, Jonas Perry. The way you come in here and invite yourself t' eat is a real sad thing."

"He didn't invite himself, Aunt. I asked him so I could chew him out some more for this afternoon. This is *punishment*." Chad's eyes belied the serious tone of his voice.

The little man looked hungrily at the baked potatoes and buttery green beans already on the table. "I'll take my lickin' like a man soon's I get on the outside of this food. You got a right sharp tongue, Clara, but yer the best cook in town."

Flushing at the unexpected compliment, Clara allowed Chad to seat her. "What all happened this afternoon, besides Sock playing his terrible tricks on Sabina?''

Deciding to keep Chad in the spotlight, Sabina said brightly, ''Chad gave us a lesson in creative expression. I learned some wonderful new combinations of great cusswords.''

''In front of Erica!''

''Jonas let your granddaughter sweet-talk him into letting her operate the front-end loader. Our lady inspector went along for the ride.''

His voice was again deceptively soft, and Sabina realized Chad hadn't forgiven anyone involved in the afternoon's adventure. She plunged in. ''Chad doesn't think a woman should drive a loader. He wouldn't even look at my operating licenses.''

Her imagination caught, Clara's mouth pursed thoughtfully before she turned to her nephew. ''If Sabina knows how, what's wrong with Erica learnin'? The business buys her bread and butter, don't it?''

Chad wouldn't back down. ''It would also pay for her funeral if she were killed. She had no business out there today.'' How could he explain his concern without sounding like a complete fool? He said to Sabina, ''Before you run any of our stuff, I want to check you out. Sometimes those permits are issued too quickly.''

''I'm sure the mining company I worked for in Colorado would appreciate your skepticism, Chad. The two years I worked there, I operated everything they had.''

Chad grinned, then answered, ''I like to think of myself as properly cautious. My sister Eden is a structural engineer, in case you're interested. We've had these little discussions several times." His mouth tightened. "It frightens me to think of her dancing along bare girders with only a hard hat for protection. If I pretend she's a librarian, I sleep better."

Now it was Jonas's turn to grin. "Yer just gettin' fearful in your old age, Chad. Y'need a wife and family to give ya somethin' to *really* worry about."

Chad made the expected rude response, then centered his attention on the rack of spareribs on his plate.

"That's funny. My brother *is* a librarian," Sabina interjected quickly. "I bought him a hard hat for protection from falling books while he superintends his library's move into a new building. Some of the volunteers are overenthusiastic."

The front door slammed. Clara rose as if on strings. "There's Daniel. His dinner's warm in the kitchen."

As she bustled out, Daniel bounded in from the hall. His hair was damp from his shower; his fair skin glowed with health. Sabina was struck again by the twins' blond good looks.

"Terrible practice. *Terrible!*" he complained cheerfully as he fell into the chair at her side.

Chad eyed him skeptically. "Should I change my bet on tomorrow night's game?"

Daniel reassured his cousin. "Every time we have a lousy practice before a big game, we win going away. Coach really tore a strip off us before we left."

"When ya' leavin' tomorrow?" Jonas asked.

"Right after first period. Coach wants us on campus for a short practice to get used to the floor, and then an early meal. Playing a seven o'clock game is the pits.'' Daniel eyed the heaped plate Clara set in front of him. ''Thanks, Gran. This is my favorite.''

''Just so's you play good tomorrow night.'' She watched each bite he took, as if assuring herself of his nourishment.

Mystified, Sabina watched Daniel attack his food. Finally, she asked, ''Is this a special game?''

''The regional basketball finals are in Athens. Sunday's winner will be one of the final eight teams in the state. The town will be empty tomorrow night,'' Chad explained.

''Then I'll leave early so I won't delay you. I'm nearly finished, anyway.'' The idea of leaving this warm family circle made Sabina feel bereft. She wished she could help Erica before she left. Could Chad really be such a hard-core chauvinist?

She needed distance. Sitting across the table from Chad put stress on her nervous system. He looked as if he could read her mind as he said, ''You're welcome to stay over and go with us if you like. I'm sure I could turn up another ticket.''

The invitation stole her appetite. When everyone at the table seconded the offer she felt even worse. ''I really have to get back. I have a . . . a Saturday dentist appointment.''

Chad threw her a skeptical look, but commented, ''That sounds like fun.''

Daniel finished inhaling his meal and pushed his chair back. ''I better hit the books for that test first period." He threw perfunctory farewells behind him as he headed for the den.

"See? I told you the boy ain't been actin' right." Clara said worriedly.

"Consarn it, woman! What's funny about wantin' to get his book work done?" Jonas glowered at Clara. "You women think a boy has to be makin' sense all the time. He's het up about this game tomorra, and that's the end of it."

Clara glared back at her longtime adversary. "What do you know about boys, you old goat? Old bachelors like you should be put to pasture when they start thinkin' they know anythin'. I say the boy's holdin' somethin' back. He don't seem as excited as he should be." She looked at Chad, who stifled a sigh and stood.

"I'm sure there's nothing wrong, but I don't want you worrying. He's at a rough age." The frown creasing his forehead eased as he asked Sabina, "Sure we can finish up tomorrow?"

"No problem. If we start early, I'll be gone by noon." Sabina wanted to escape Chad's clear golden gaze, which seemed to pin her against the polished wood of her chair.

"Then I'll pick you up here at seven. Has anybody heard a weather report?"

"Mebbe some rain tomorrow, Chad. Nothin' to be a problem," Jonas reassured. " 'Tain't that far to Athens anyway."

Chad's departure made the room seem empty, and Sabina helped Clara clear the table. Recalling her promise to Erica, she hoped Chad's talk with Daniel didn't last long.

After refusing an invitation to help wash dishes, Jonas left. Clara, pink-cheeked, seemed revved by their skirmish. She saw Sabina's quizzical survey, and turned even pinker. "Jonas and I nearly got married about fifty years ago. He called it off. Said I was too 'managin'.' I never let him forget it."

Her high color and the militance in her eyes were nearly Sabina's undoing. The slam of the front door reverberating through the house enabled her to stifle her laughter.

"See? He won't talk to Chad. I 'spect Chad didn't go about it right." Concern chased the color from the older woman's face.

"Would it hurt if I just stopped in to wish Daniel good luck?" Sabina wished she could escape the webs of involvement these nice people were wrapping around her. The sticky filaments felt as if they would entangle her permanently.

Clara brightened. "Your pretty face might just bring him 'round. He won't dare send you packin'."

As she made her way to the cozy den, Sabina thought, *I just want to give him Erica's message and get away.* Before this, she had always managed to keep others at arm's length. She wasn't accustomed to people sharing their problems, their pasts, and their hopes for the future. The thing that disturbed her most was that she cared.

Chapter Six

The silence in the den was otherworldly. Pearl Jam held court; Sabina could see the empty CD case on the floor next to the table. She was grateful headphones confined the sound to Daniel. After this afternoon's explosion, rock music would complete the destruction of her nervous system.

Standing across the table from the teenager, she waved her hand between his face and the open book in front of him. No response. She touched his hand gently and felt her heart constrict with compassion for his all-too-visible vulnerability. Daniel had the body of an oversize adult, but the finishing process hadn't yet taken place.

Daniel reacted by removing the headphones with polite reluctance. "Did you need something, Sabina?"

Aware no one but he could hear her, Sabina whispered, "There's mail for you in the window seat. Erica made me swear I wouldn't tell anyone but you."

Before she finished speaking, Daniel rushed to the bay window and pulled out the thick envelope. As Sabina turned to leave, his voice, young and pleading, stopped her. "Please. Would you mind staying while

I open this? It may be the most important letter of my life, and I need someone with me.''

Dear Heaven. I'm trapped again, Sabina moaned inwardly. She'd never before become involved with people she scarcely knew. Caring made her feel vulnerable.

Daniel's fingers made a long project of opening the broad flap. By the time he removed the contents, Sabina wanted to shout, *Get on with it!*

''They want me,'' he said prayerfully, his eyes moving over the letter. Tears of joy glistened in his eyes as he dropped the watermarked stationery on the table and swept Sabina off her feet in a gigantic bear hug.

''Whatever the news is, it must be good,'' she managed to gasp when he set her down.

His hands shaking, Daniel picked up the letter and handed it to her. ''Read.''

She scanned the page once, then twice. ''A full scholarship! The Columbus College of Art and Design! Daniel, that's unbelievable! Do you know how hard it is just to get accepted there?'' Her voice quivered with laughter as she added, ''Of course you do. How stupid of me.''

Then she realized the implications. ''You're supposed to attend the Colorado School of Mines! How will Chad take this?''

Her words weren't really a question. They were a gloomy, self-contained statement.

The joy drained visibly from Daniel's face. His voice was tight as he answered, ''I'll just have to choose the right time to tell him. He *has* to understand. He just has to.''

Sabina's heart contracted. For the second time in one day, she found herself listening to another person's hopes and dreams, this time the second of a pair of twins. For one dizzy moment, she wondered if that could be considered only one personal life.

For someone who had lived a lifetime avoiding emotional involvement, things were moving too fast. Sabina's mother had been dedicated to her accounting career, and her father was devoted to his philosophy classes at the university. She and her brother Jack had been raised as miniature adults. No scenes, no emotional outbursts ever disturbed their family life.

Until this moment, she had never wondered how her remote parents had ever married and produced children.

Then she recalled her own broken engagement. Things had ended when she realized she and John had no passion for each other. She'd had a sudden, searing vision of life that offered only tepid friendship. The boy's desperation touched something deep inside her. She had never experienced caring until she came to this rural area in eastern Ohio.

"Daniel, can I do anything? I'm not sure Chad would listen to me, but maybe I can sort of . . . pave the way a little?"

Sinking into his chair, Daniel shook his head. "Nobody's ever been kinder to me in my whole life than Chad. Eric and I would have crawled into a cave and died after Mom and Dad were killed, but he wouldn't let us. Sometimes he just sat and held us. He goes to our teachers' conferences. And to PTA meetings.''

A picture of Chad at a PTA meeting flashed through Sabina's mind. She could see him, probably in a banker's suit like the one he'd worn the other evening, prowling around with that effortless grace of his, looking as out of place as a tiger lily in a field of soybeans. The mothers present probably averaged a forty percent rise in their aggregate blood pressure. Sabina's voice cracked as she said, ''PTA meetings?''

''He was president year before last. Then the banks and the mining company began to need more time and attention. A year or so ago he started to . . . to pull away a little. Now he leaves town every once in a while.'' Daniel grinned. ''Calls it R and R. Gran says he goes away to sow his wild oats. He's still here for us, but he lets us make more of our own decisions.''

Without thinking, Sabina snapped, ''According to your grandmother, he sometimes brings part of the oat field home.''

Daniel's grin widened. ''He only did that once, and Gran nearly had a cow. Erica and I laughed till we were sick. That was one foxy chick . . . a real city girl.'' He peered up at her. ''Does that bother you? Gran said there are hormones stewing between you two.''

Sabina straightened, color flooding her cheeks. ''I'm here on state business, remember? Besides, even if there were something between us, that's nothing to do with your problem.''

''I just thought I'd take a sounding.'' He grinned, looking about thirteen, then became serious again. ''I can't do anything about the scholarship this week. When the time is right, Erica and I'll tackle him together. It's not as if I'd be leaving him in the lurch or anything like that. If Erica weren't so hot to take over, I'd never even consider this, no matter how much my art means to me.'' The determination in his voice indicated he'd given the matter deep thought before he'd applied for the scholarship. ''The thing is, she'd be terrific.''

Waving a final farewell to her lifetime habit of detachment, Sabina said, ''You may be right. And you shouldn't even consider letting your talent go to waste.''

''I sure feel better talking to someone besides Erica about this. We've worn each other out.'' He glanced at the table in front of him. ''I'd better hit the books so I don't flunk that physics test first thing tomorrow. Can you imagine a teacher giving a test the morning of the big game?''

Her concern eased by his return to normalcy, Sabina wanted only to put distance between herself and the turmoil of the Kincaid twins. ''Are you a good basketball player?''

''When I'm on, I'm the hottest thing on the floor.''

His confident reply rang in Sabina's ears as she pulled her striped flannel granny gown over her head. Some indefinable quality about the twins drew her, making her care desperately for their dreams. She slipped her feet into fluffy pink slippers. Too much had happened today, and her mind was in a whirl.

When had she last been ready for bed at nine in the evening?

A quick rummage through her suitcase located several paperbacks she carried for emergencies. The choice between a romance and a mystery was easy— she could do without romantic stimulation. Chad Peters already stirred her hormones past the comfort zone. Besides, the Dorothy Grimes was one she'd missed.

Curling up on the small couch, she pulled the woolly afghan over her shoulders and tucked it around her lap, then forced her thoughts to the printed page.

Half an hour later, a persistent tapping penetrated her absorption. After several moments she pinpointed the source, narrowing it down to the corner of the room. "That must be the private entrance Mrs. Kincaid mentioned. I've been so busy I never even noticed that door," she murmured.

Clutching the afghan around her shoulders, she padded to the door, certain of her caller's identity and half afraid to respond. Her heart thumped against her ribs. "Who is it?"

"It's the Phantom of the Hills." Chad's voice was readily recognizable through the double barrier of wood and storm door. "Let me in."

Mumbling beneath her breath, her hands shaking, Sabina fumbled with the chain and catch. As she eased the door open, Chad stepped inside, bringing with him a gust of frigid fresh air.

"Turning cold," he said, blowing on his bare hands.

Sabina saw his unrepentant grin. She suspected his visit had nothing to do with the weather, which he probably thought was a credible excuse for his aunt, should she discover him.

"Shut that door before I freeze. What do you think you're doing, sneaking in the back way?" The flannel gown offered little protection against the cold air. The tremor in her knees had nothing to do with the temperature, yet she forced herself to pretend his presence had no effect on her. She wondered if fate were conspiring with him.

Chad leaned against the closed door as he unsnapped his down vest. "You really know how to make a man feel welcome. I went to a lot of trouble to avoid disturbing everyone else in the house."

"Particularly since you knew your Aunt Clara would say, 'Behave yourself, Chad,' and particularly since you knew I'd assume there was some important reason for you to come back at this time of night." Sabina forced herself to meet his teasing eyes coolly. "Is there a change in tomorrow's schedule?" She watched his comprehensive glance take in the pink-striped gown, saw the incredulous widening of his eyes when he spotted the fluffy slippers. Her fingers clutched the afghan tighter.

"No changes. We'll still visit that last reclaimed site after breakfast, then finish up in the office. That wasn't why I came back."

She had always thought of herself as capable of organized thought. Now her mind was full of wild imaginings. Chad pushed himself away from the door and closed the space between them.

"I came back for another taste. This morning wasn't enough." With devastating care, Chad unfolded her clutching fingers one by one from the afghan until it fell to the floor.

He placed her freed hands inside his vest, pressing them against his chest. "This time I'm not in as much of a hurry."

The sweetness of his brief kiss melted Sabina. She yielded, leaning into the hand which had moved to cup the side of her head, letting her fingers burrow against the knit of his sweater. She nestled against his palm, smiling dreamily against his callused fingers.

"You're very sweet."

His softly spoken words had the same effect on Sabina as an ice cube down her back. "What am I doing?" she demanded. She pulled away from him. "I never do things like this! How could I forget I'm here officially?" The golden heat in his eyes told her exactly why she'd committed such a lapse. What she saw there mirrored her own feelings.

Surprise spread over Chad's face, almost as if he welcomed her panic. He teased, "You mean you don't do this with all the mine managers, so you can blackmail them?"

"Don't be absurd. You're . . . a surprise. Sort of like finding a wild card in a poker hand." She couldn't attach too much importance to his kisses; she couldn't let him know how deeply shaken she was. Telling her quivering insides to behave, Sabina sparred, "I already asked you whether you made a big move on all the deputy inspectors who come your way.''

''You're the first lady they've sent. If there are more who look and smell like you, I might make it a habit.''

''What a comfort. I think.''

Chad's smile was devastating as he moved closer. ''Are you saying you want exclusive rights?''

''Just stay where you are.''

''Shucks, ma'am. You're no fun at all.''

She folded her arms across her chest and glared at him. Sabina had never known anyone could joke about something which affected her this profoundly, but here she was, quivering within while bandying innuendos—and wearing nothing but a flannel granny gown.

Sabina snatched the afghan from the floor and flung it around her shoulders. ''I'll show you fun if you don't get out of here this minute. A good shout will bring your aunt on the run. Then what will happen?''

Sighing, Chad resnapped his vest. ''She already suspects I'm past redemption. You tasted even better the second time, you know.''

''Get out.''

''You're sure you don't want me to tuck you in?''

Ignoring the wistful expression on his face, she repeated her order. This time he left.

The encounter replayed itself in her mind long into the night. Sabina's common sense told her she couldn't get involved with a man who was part playboy, part chauvinist, and a surface miner. Chad was nothing but trouble. Besides, he was probably just amusing himself, livening up a dreary winter.

She'd go back to Columbus, get on with her job, and forget him. With any luck, a year or more would pass before she was sent back to Calico. By then, the situation with the twins would be worked out, and Chad would have come across someone else to charm.

Her abbreviated night's rest only enhanced Sabina's pre-coffee grumpiness, so it was doubly irritating to find Chad at the breakfast table to offer her a steaming mug before she sat down. "Don't you ever eat breakfast at home?" she grumbled disagreeably.

"My coffeepot's broken."

Clara placed a platter of bacon and golden fried mush on the table. "First I heard of it." She paused on her return to the stove to add, "A' course, if I'd known he was goin' to be here again this morning, I'd have told him to bring his toothbrush when he came back last night. He could 'a slept in the spare room upstairs."

The blush that swept Sabina's satin cheeks delighted Chad. Even though his aunt credited him with activities that never took place, he'd never been able to fool her about those that actually happened. Her prescience had unnerved him and Zack throughout their formative years.

His own mother seldom missed anything, but she had been more flexible. She also freely admitted to a far from stainless youth. This admission always brought a knowing grin to his father's face.

"I had a business question for Sabina about today's schedule."

"Monkey business is more like it. Good thing you didn't stay longer or I'd a' come down." Clara lined up a fresh row of cold, pale slices of mush in the hot frying pan as if for a photograph.

The exchange did nothing for Sabina's disposition; her coffee might as well have been Kool-Aid. She ate silently, chewing each mouthful as if it were a religious exercise. She couldn't recall ever having been so embarrassed. Did these people always bring up everything about each other's private lives for general discussion? At breakfast? Chad's entry through the private door last night must have been common knowledge. After all, she hadn't pushed him down the little flight of steps—or even protested.

"I'll tell you one thing, Aunt Clara. She missed a golden opportunity to flip me over her shoulder."

"I'd have helped her. All she had to do was call me." Clara impaled him with an accusing stare.

As much as she relished seeing Chad on the receiving end, Sabina could see he enjoyed the exchange. Before she could steer the conversation to a safer subject, the twins entered. Each seemed keyed up, and she was sure Erica had corralled her brother about his mail last night. But that meant they'd . . .

"Did you spend the night, Chad?" Erica's eyes sparkled with curiosity. "I saw your car when I got home, and wondered why you came back. You were driving the Jeep yesterday."

Daniel grinned mischievously. "He didn't come in while I was awake. Was he here to see you, Sabina?"

He threw his two hundred pounds of youthful energy into the chair beside hers.

Sabina felt overwhelmed by masculinity. Chad, his smile wicked and mature, on her right, and Daniel, still short of his potential, sprawled on her left. She wished herself a million miles away.

"Children, children. Don't you know it's rude to pry?" Chad's teasing reply answered neither question.

Sabina's mind reeled. Would he come right out and tell them he'd come back to kiss her? No one had any secrets around here, she thought, forgetting the twins' confidences. Scrambling frantically to establish her innocence, she said, "Chad had a few changes in today's schedule he wanted to alert me about."

"Hmmph. I never saw anyone turn beet-red about a schedule before." Clara slapped crisp mush on a platter and thumped it onto the middle of the table. "Eat, Erica. You'll be late."

As he filled his plate, Daniel leaned toward her and whispered, "I knew you two had a little something cooking. Go for it."

Help came from an unexpected quarter, saving Sabina from another monumental blush. "You were up pretty late the night before a big game, weren't you, Daniel?"

"He waited up for me, Chad. I . . . I had some notes for the test this morning I'd forgotten to give him." Erica completed the rescue, avoiding forbidden territory herself.

"I remember being too wired about a game to sleep," Chad reminisced. He watched the covert glances the twins exchanged, and reminded himself to get to the bottom of their secret. Something was cooking. But later, after the stress of the tournament. After the inspection. After he had settled things with Sabina. The twins' problems and the solutions were his responsibility, one he couldn't turn over to anyone else, but this time they had to stand in line.

This time he had his own dilemma. He hadn't been searching for someone like Sabina; he hadn't even been sure someone like her existed. The differences between them weren't insurmountable; they had more in common than Sabina would admit. All he had to do was convince her, which would take time. Time, which was always in short supply.

Remnants of exhilaration from the night before had brought him to his aunt's early this morning. Chad knew Clara was secretly pleased when he joined them for meals, no matter when.

As if unable to stay in her chair any longer, Sabina drained her coffee mug and stood, announcing, ''I'm going to load my car and follow you to the office this morning, Chad. I'll head straight home when we're finished, so you can leave for the game.''

She yearned for the privacy of her car, where she could regroup. Ever since she'd come to this place, control had been taken out of her hands. Sabina didn't like the unexpected, and her feelings for Chad were unnerving, unplanned. Surely the burning attraction she felt would fade when she put sixty or seventy miles between them.

"Good idea," Chad said. "That way you won't be stranded if I'm called away."

"Blast him, he didn't have to sound so pleased with himself," Sabina raged as she stuffed her toothbrush into its case. "He acts as if he knows something I don't." Sabina snatched her driving coat and dress boots from the closet. Getting back into civilized dress for the drive home would be a relief. The hard-toed boots were necessary in the field, but wearing them elsewhere offended her feminine instincts.

Loading her car took only minutes. All that remained was settling her bill with Clara Kincaid, a task that was every bit as difficult as she'd expected. "You'll never make any money at this if you tell perfect strangers you were just glad for their company. Besides, the state expects me to turn in a voucher for my expenses," she said.

"You'd better get out your receipt book, Aunt Clara. You could be accused of furnishing hospitality to the person who puts us out of business. She might think it's a bribe," Chad teased.

"I guess I can say who I charge and who I don't. It's been a real joy to have you, Sabina. Are you sure you have to pay?"

Sabina felt a stinging sensation behind her eyes. She would miss the homey comfort of the Kincaid household. Not the home, but the people. She'd probably never see them again. Clara's no-nonsense warmth would be extended to the next person offered the comfort of the tiny suite. Sabina Hanlon would be forgotten.

She should be glad to escape the tentacles of involvement Chad and the Kincaids had wrapped around her. Everyone here would have to solve their own problems and live with the results. They had no bearing on her. She was going back to Columbus and her job. Just because for once she'd come across people who cared enough to mine properly didn't mean there weren't others out there who were careless, and she intended to track them down.

Clara took several minutes to locate a dog-eared receipt book and decide on a figure. Sabina decided not to protest the low rate, knowing that even *that* was charged under duress. Arguing was not her style, and at this point she wanted to leave as gracefully as possible.

She returned Clara's brisk hug, feeling a surge of genuine affection for the older woman. ''I can't thank you enough, even though I probably gained five pounds. I appreciate the recipes.''

''When you come back, I'll fix some real special things. I didn't know you were coming, or I'd a' been ready.''

Sabina smiled regretfully. ''I probably won't return until Calico opens a new site. Maybe not even then. If I should come this direction, I'll stop by.'' *Much as I'd love to see you, I won't be back,* she thought. She couldn't become further involved with these people. As for Chad, if she had to return, she'd somehow make sure he was out of town on one of his little R and Rs when she arrived.

Clara smiled. "You do that. I'll be real glad to see you."

As she started her car, Chad tapped on the window, motioning for her to lower the glass. He leaned in the opening. "I have a stop to make on the way. Here's the key to the office. You go on in and keep warm until I get there."

Chad's brief intrusion left the imprint of his personality on the interior of the state car, as if a shade of his presence had taken possession of the seat next to her. Hoping to eradicate the image of that flashing smile, she popped her Mozart tape into the tape deck. If Mozart couldn't rout the imprint of Chad Peters's personality, she was in trouble.

Chapter Seven

Minutes after she arrived at the office, Chad pulled up.

"Hop in. This won't take long." He glanced at the sullen sky. "I hope the snow doesn't arrive early. The radio predicted a storm by mid afternoon, but snow's tough to forecast."

As she climbed in beside him, the breathlessness she had begun to take for granted seized Sabina. "Jonas said rain."

"He did, but the cold front shifted."

"If you want to leave early for Athens, don't feel you're abandoning me. I can finish up in the office by myself. I promise not to carry off any secret papers."

Chad dashed her hopes. "Plenty of time. I want you safely on your way home before this hits. And with this inspection out of the way, I can celebrate after the game with a clear conscience."

The Jeep lurched into a pothole, throwing her against his shoulder. Sabina's hasty attempt to pull away drew a crooked grin from Chad. His grin widened wolfishly before he added, "Of course, my conscience doesn't have to be *spotless*."

Ignoring his remark, Sabina said, "You're awfully confident . . . about the game, I mean."

"That shade of pink on your cheeks is flattering, Sabina." The Jeep swung wide around another curve, this time throwing her against the door. "But you're right. I'm sure we'll win."

If he talked about basketball, he surely wouldn't make any references to last night. She had to get back to the haven of her apartment. There were too many entanglements here.

She wondered if it was already too late.

"This is a good place to stop. Look down there."

She was so immersed in her thoughts that Chad's voice startled her. He'd pulled off into a small clearing at the top of a low ridge. By swiveling her head she could easily follow the direction he indicated.

Roughly half the shallow valley had been plowed the previous fall and lay ready for spring. A fence of bare-branched young shrubs backed by new fencing divided the land. "What will the rest be used for?"

"Pasture. The owner leased the mineral rights beneath his dairy farm to get enough money to survive," Chad said flatly. "Zack mined it in halves over two years so he could maintain his farming."

Forgetting she didn't want to meet his eyes, Sabina swung around to face him. "I suppose he owed your bank money."

"Mine and several others. This was the only way he could keep the land his grandfather farmed." Before she could respond angrily, he laid his fingers over her mouth. "Farming is a harsh life, Sabina. A new government regulation, one dry summer, or a wet one, and things can turn against you.''

She pushed his hand from her lips. "But you used him!''

Chad ran the rejected fingers through his hair before closing his eyes wearily. *"He* came to *me.* I referred him to Zack. That's the last site Zack mined before he died.'' When he opened his eyes, she saw his intensity. "We take care of our own around here. The farmer's pride would accept this kind of help. In the end, we were all better off.''

"But that's . . .''

"It's called survival.'' Chad's voice was hard. "Do you know what it's like to lose not only the land you inherited but the only way you know to make a living? What career change is a dairy farmer supposed to make? Can he become a computer programmer? A doctor? He and his family can't survive on what he'd make working in a fast-food place.''

The truth of his words struck Sabina like a slap. Her idealism had never allowed her to look further than the effects on the land. Before she'd come here, everything was black or white. She knew industry needed the energy coal provided. What she despised was the method used to get the coal. Until now, she'd blamed the mining companies.

She'd never looked at things from the perspective of Chad's anonymous dairy farmer. And he still owned his land. Wasn't this beautiful site what she thought of as the ideal result?

"I've never thought of it that way. No one's ever

presented the other side. Thank you.'' The admission hurt, but she was ruthlessly honest about such things. She felt as if a large chip had just fallen from her shoulder.

He smiled. ''You're a very up-front lady. For the second time in two days, you've conceded a point.''

''I'm sure every site isn't mined because of hardship,'' she reminded him.

Chad shifted gears and gunned the engine. ''I'd have been disappointed if you hadn't noticed that. What's the old phrase? 'Two sides to every story.' There are as many reasons as there are people involved. And as many poorly executed mines.''

The roar of the Jeep's engine drowned out her reply. By the time they reached the office, Sabina's mind had focused on the weather. She threw an anxious glance at the sullen sky. ''That's getting ugly.''

''We'll work fast,'' Chad agreed. ''I promise to stick to business.''

Studiously ignoring him, Sabina greeted Edna and headed straight for the office, Sock hugging her steps like a shadow. She threw her coat over a chair and opened her briefcase. She would finish her work and leave. ''Okay, let's see those surveyors' results and the report on the quality of the runoff.''

Edna appeared in the doorway, her hands gripped together. ''Chad . . . that Mr. Merton called. Just before you came. He . . . he said he was coming here.''

''When, Edna?'' Chad's gentle voice didn't match his frown nor the steely look in his eyes.

''He . . . he just drove up.''

The sound of the front door closing elicited a soft epithet from Chad. "Thanks, Edna. Tell him I'll be right out." He turned to Sabina. "I'll get those papers for you." He went to the filing cabinet in the corner and extracted a file.

The door didn't latch behind him. As the conversation drifted through the opening, Sabina moved to close it. The stranger's words froze her in place.

"You're a hard man to catch, Mr. Peters. I apologize for coming without an appointment, but my principal is offering terms that are very favorable to the Calico heirs."

Chad's reply was unintelligible, as if he lowered his voice in hope of bringing his visitor's volume down.

"I quite understand your inability to talk now. Can we have lunch next week? Perhaps Wednesday?"

He must have received a negative. Sabina heard a note of desperation in the visitor's voice. "Then Thursday."

Sabina strained to hear Chad's reply, then realized she was shamelessly eavesdropping. By the time he returned, she was hard at work.

Two hours later, Sabina pushed aside papers and stretched. Chad hadn't mentioned his conversation with the unseen Merton, and there was no way she could ask him about it. She reminded herself for the tenth time that the whole thing was none of her business.

Other than interruptions for telephone calls, he had been all business. Of course, he was anxious to get away. Why was she suspicious? Her eyes wandered to the table in the corner where Chad labored over a stack of printouts.

Light from the brass table lamp highlighted his lean cheek and brought the thick brush of his lashes into sharp relief. How ridiculous for a man to have doll's lashes, thick and blunt.

Sabina shook her head to clear it. There was no future for her with Chad.

The room suddenly seemed too small, as if the walls were closing in. "Do you mind if I open the door? It's getting awfully close in here." Sabina rose jerkily, hiding her inner desperation, and pulled the door inward. The light coming from the spacious outer office was diffused, as if dependent for illumination on the plastic panels set into the ceiling. The room looked as if it were late evening.

Turning, she recrossed the office and opened the blinds. The view forced a strangled sound from her throat. She jumped when Chad's hand fell reassuringly on her shoulder.

"I should have known this storm would come fast and hit hard. March weather's impossible to predict."

Chad neglected to share the fact that an hour earlier he'd authorized the managers to close the banks and ordered the mine site cleared. His conscience was clear. He'd told her earlier about the forecast. He just hadn't mentioned that experience had taught him to recognize a fast-moving front.

A sheet of white swirled in front of their eyes, obscuring all but the vague outlines of two mammoth machines parked no more than twenty feet from the building. Bending closer to the glass, Sabina inspected the snow-laden branches of the low shrub growing beneath the window. "There are already over four inches of snow! When did that happen?"

"I'd say in the past hour or so," Chad said. "The roads will be impassable in half an hour, if they aren't already."

He regretted missing the game. On the other hand, he might never have another chance to get to know Sabina better. The business part of her visit was finished; Chad hated to mix business with pleasure.

The slam of the front door echoed hollowly through the building, bringing a gust of cold air with it. A voice said urgently, "Edna, you've got to leave now, or we'll end up spending the night here."

"Edna's father is right. We all have to get out of here." Chad locked the spreadsheets in a drawer. "Get your stuff. We can make it to town in the Jeep."

"But I have to get back to Columbus tonight." Panic quavered in Sabina's voice.

Chad gathered the papers from his desk and stowed them in her open briefcase. "You have no business setting out in this. These fast, short storms catch the road crews with their pants down, and things will get worse as you travel west. Come back to Aunt Clara's. These blow in fast and melt the next day. Until then, you're stuck."

Sabina's common sense was stronger than her panic at the thought of being snowbound with Chad. After a second despairing look out the window, she gathered her belongings.

Chad joined Edna and her father in the reception room, and Sabina heard their voices as she zipped her parka and pulled up her hood. The door slammed, and Chad returned, snapping his vest. "Sam says the roads are all right if we take our time."

"Is that all you're wearing? Don't you have a hat or something?" He looked poorly prepared for the weather outside.

"I can last for eight miles. Maybe the heater will decide to work." He reached for her briefcase. "We'll put your luggage in the Jeep."

"I'll follow you. My car has front-wheel drive." If she was to be snowed in, she wanted to be ready for instant flight.

Chad shrugged and switched off the light. "If you insist." He led the way to the parking lot and helped her clear the windshield before they set out.

As she followed the barely discernible tracks of the Jeep, snow tugged at her wheels, as if willing the car toward the ditches on either side of the road. Visibility was nonexistent. Escape to the haven of her apartment was out of the question. Clara would be there, and probably Erica, but even that was inadequate protection against the attraction tugging at her.

Sabina did the only thing she could think of. She prayed for a rapid thaw.

Her petitions continued until they slithered into the wide driveway. So great was her concentration that she nearly neglected to stop. She wondered if prayer would be an acceptable excuse for wrecking a state-owned automobile.

Clara opened the front door of the house before Sabina could tug out her bags. ''I was hopin' you'd come back,'' the older woman said as she hurried them into the warm hall. ''I knew when this started it would be a real ripsnorter. We'll have to listen to the game on the radio. That Billy Parker don't describe it so's you'd know what's goin' on, but at least he gives the score. Chad, you wipe off that dog before he heads for Daniel's room,'' she ordered as Sock slipped into the house.

Shaking the snow from his vest, Chad reached for the dog's collar and explained, ''The announcer from the local station tries hard, but the commentary gets a little confused at times.'' He looked at Clara. ''I take it the team got off all right.''

''Daniel just called to say the other team got there, too. The university'll put 'em all up tonight. Whenever you're ready, come out to the kitchen and eat.''

Erica joined them as Clara was ladling fragrant chili into thick pottery bowls. ''I can't stand it. If they'd let the pep club leave with the team, I'd be there. Who wants to listen to silly Billy Parker?'' She threw herself into her chair.

''Beats bein' stuck in a ditch somewhere,'' said Clara, thumping a bowl in front of her granddaughter.

Glancing beneath her lashes, Sabina was struck by Chad's bland expression. ''Chad told me the same thing about starting out for Columbus. I wish I'd kept a better eye on the weather.''

Distracted from her own disappointment, Erica asked, ''What's the rush? Hot date tonight?''

Without looking up, Chad answered, "A dentist appointment tomorrow. Some people actually enjoy root canals and Novocain."

Sabina refused to rise to his bait. "I simply don't want to impose on you people any longer than I have to."

"She's afraid she might have a good time." Chad cut a generous piece of corn bread and slathered it with butter. "Maybe she doesn't know being snowed in is an art in this part of the country, social life being what it is."

Giggles swept Erica. "Remember two years ago when we played Monopoly all night? I had two hotels on every piece of property I owned, and more money than all of you and the bank combined."

"I think that was when you got butter from the popcorn all over the money because you counted your ill-gotten gains every ten minutes. We had to buy a new set," Chad grumbled.

Erica retorted, "You should have known better than to sell me Park Place so early in the game."

"You cheated," he said flatly, his eyes twinkling.

"Did not."

"Stop your branglin'," Clara intervened. "A body couldn't tell which of you was grown up."

"I've heard enough to know I'm not playing Monopoly tonight," Sabina asserted. "Sounds as if you play for blood."

Chad scooped up the last of his chili, promising, "I'm sure we'll find something to do. *After* the game, of course. There are all kinds of ways to celebrate."

He rose from the table in one lithe movement. "I'm going to join Sock in Daniel's room. I need to make up the sleep I lost last night."

"Hmph. If you'd stayed home, instead of bothering Christian folk, you'd have gotten a decent night's rest."

Chad threw his arm up in mock self-defense and headed jauntily out the door.

"Just like the pigs. Eat and take a nap," his aunt said.

"He can't hear you, Gran." Erica turned to Sabina and explained, "She simply adores him, but she never likes to let him get too sure of himself."

Sabina wondered what it would be like to be loved so much you could laugh off criticism. Her mother's efforts to make her perfect hadn't succeeded. She'd been adequate at ballet and pedestrian at piano, but had excelled in sports and in class. Her mother had taken the successes for granted and looked on the failures as lack of effort. Her father hadn't noticed anything.

Until now, the fight to preserve the environment had consumed her idealism. Chad's explanation of rural economics this morning still haunted her.

"I think I'll carry my things back to my room and shed a few layers of clothing," she said.

"Mind if I come along for some girl talk?" Erica fell in behind her.

Sabina soon discovered Erica wanted more than idle chatter. "I've thought about what you said. Tell me about your job."

Later, Sabina wondered how Chad could be oblivious to his cousin's obsession with taking over Calico. The girl already knew more about the work, the rules and regulations, and the management than some people already in the business. All Erica needed was schooling and experience.

"I can't encourage you, Erica. You'll meet Chad head-on over this." She cared more than she'd thought possible. "I don't want to be the cause of a family uproar." *Or your disappointment if Chad sells Calico.*

"You mean you don't want Chad to think you encouraged me." Erica sent her mentor a sparkling glance. "He's totally hung up on you. Do you think he worried about *my* neck yesterday? Fat chance! He was shaken right down to his steel toes over *you*. He wasn't afraid the state would take revenge. That was just a good excuse."

Careful to control her expression, Sabina said firmly, "You're reading things into this, Erica."

"Cop-out, Sabina. You two are wired whenever you're together. Chad could've called last night about schedules. There's a telephone over there on the table. *I* think he came because he thought he'd get a 'fix' from the sight of you," she said, grinning cheekily.

The humor of the situation struck Sabina, and she giggled. She still wasn't accustomed to open discussions of private lives. "I . . . I'm not used to such bluntness, Erica."

"You'll learn. I have a feeling we're going to see a lot of you around here."

A loud thump on the door of the tiny apartment

rescued Sabina from further embarrassment. "Come in!" she called, unwilling to drag herself from the depths of the couch.

Sock forced his way through the opening, wriggling in ecstasy as he threw himself on Erica's reclining figure. Chad followed, looking rested and pleased with the world in general. "This is a textbook March blizzard. Either of you want to bet the roads will be clear by noon tomorrow?"

Sabina looked at her watch. Had she and Erica been talking for two hours? The blanket of white outside had wrapped them in a silent cocoon where time was suspended.

"I need volunteers to bring in firewood. Aunt Clara's unearthing the popcorn popper and baking beans. We're going to roast hot dogs." Chad sounded as enthusiastic as a small boy looking forward to a day off from school.

A light dawned in Sabina's mind as Erica set off in search of her coat and boots. "You're enjoying this too much. Did you suspect the storm would arrive so soon?"

"The signs were there if you knew what to look for. Aunt Clara could have told you, if you'd asked."

"You missed the game just so you could get snowed in?"

He didn't even have the grace to blush. His little-boy grin was disarming. "They'll win tonight. I'll see an even better game Sunday, but the chance to be snowbound with you won't turn up again, at least this winter."

Before Sabina could recover from his frankness, Clara spoke from behind him. "The boy's always been too ornery to live with honest folk." She eased past him, a fat satin bundle in her arms. "I brought you this comforter in case the 'lectricity goes off."

"Aunt Clara, if that happens, we'll have to huddle in front of the fire for warmth. I personally volunteer to make sure Sabina doesn't get chilled," Chad said.

Reaching for the comforter, Sabina frowned at him. "I prefer this, thank you. After the way you tricked me into being stuck here, I certainly wouldn't count on you to behave."

"Met your match, nephew," Clara said before she bustled back to her kitchen.

"Are you my match, Sabina?"

The light question belied the seriousness in his eyes. The walls of the room felt as if they were closing in, and Sabina struggled against the tug of his voice.

"Are we going out for wood or not?" Erica demanded from the dining room.

The spell broken, Sabina pushed past him. "You two bring it to the door, and I'll carry it to the fireplace. I'm not going back out into that mess again."

"Fair enough," Erica said. "Chad and I'll bring the wood to the service porch. Put it in that tin washtub in the den."

Chapter Eight

Later, Chad lounged to one side of the fire, pretending exhaustion from building the fire, and watching Sabina's graceful movements as she set out food.

"Put the radio on, Gran. The game starts in five minutes," Erica said, nearly dropping the meat in the fire in her excitement. "I hope Daniel makes so many baskets tonight the Celtics recruit him straight from high school."

"Don't get so het up. Last week he couldn't hit Lake Erie with a broom," Clara said.

Chad located the local station while the others filled their plates and settled about the room. It seemed natural, once he'd collected his own meal, to lower himself next to Sabina where she curled against a big cushion. The heady scent of jasmine blended with the piercing sweetness of the burning applewood.

Sabina watched the flickering shadows of the flames on the paneled walls. There had been a beautiful fireplace in the home in which she'd grown up; she remembered fires during the holidays. Early each January her mother had removed the ashes and scrubbed the grate. "This is wonderful. My mother said soot and sparks made a mess. I must have been sixteen before I realized you could make a fire whenever you felt like it.''

"We have fires for no reason at all, even in July, if it's cool," Erica said, as if unable to comprehend otherwise.

The admission was no surprise to Chad. Sabina's passion for rules and regulations had to come from somewhere. But whatever her past, Sabina had merged with his family as if she'd lived with them all her life. "Quiet. There's the toss-up."

By halftime, Daniel had scored fifteen points. "This is no contest. We're ahead by twenty points. I told you next week's game would be more of a challenge," Chad exulted.

Erica eyed him slyly. "You act as if you'd planned the storm so you could keep Sabina here."

Clara's laughter completed Sabina's embarrassment. Even as her cheeks flamed, she realized there was no malice involved in the affectionate teasing, and Chad was laughing in response. He had edged closer, and she felt mirth shake his body.

"You're just mad school was dismissed before the booster bus could leave," Chad teased.

"No, I'm jealous because I have to watch you romance Sabina."

"Hush, child." Clara raised the radio's volume. "The second half's 'bout t' start."

The outcome of the game was never in doubt, nor was the winner of the poker game which followed. Chad had a mountain of chips, while the others nursed several small stacks. "Too bad we're not playing for money, or even pieces of clothing," he said smugly. He gathered the colorful plastic heap from the middle of the table with a careless gesture, his eyes golden and teasing.

"What a thing to say to your aunt!" Clara's eyes sparkled.

"Why, Aunt Clara, you're a good-looking woman. Jonas mentioned it just the other day. Should I ask his intentions?"

Though her color heightened, Clara protested his statement. "That Jonas. If you're goin' t' make up stories, I'd best get on up t' bed. I hope Daniel can get home tomorrow."

Obeying the hint in Chad's eye, Erica yawned widely. "I'm going up too, Gran. Why does doing nothing make a person tired?"

"Close the draft before you come up, Chad. Don't keep Sabina up too late."

Chad's hand shot out, staying Sabina's attempt to rise. "Don't worry about a thing, Aunt. I'll even tuck her in." He flinched as Sabina's shoe made contact with his shin.

Wrenching her arm free from Chad's warm fingers, Sabina said, "If you leave him here with me, you may have to bandage his wounds in the morning."

"He's always been able to tend to himself, dear." The words floated back over Clara's shoulder.

"I love bloodshed and violence. Can I stay and watch?" Erica asked.

"Go to bed, brat."

Sabina wanted to run. The evening had been a delight; she couldn't remember laughing so much. Now Chad's firm declaration of intent and Clara's unexpected aiding and abetting made her nervous.

Chad rose from the card table and wrapped his warm fingers around her wrist. He tugged her to her feet. "No need to panic. I just want to talk, and maybe snuggle a little bit, until the fire dies down. This is a good night for snuggling, and it may be my last chance for a while. The snow's stopped."

"Do you think I'll be able to get home tomorrow?"

He framed her face with his hands, looking at her intently. "Are you really that eager to leave?"

"Yes. No. I don't know." Her eyelids fell, the spread of lashes dark against her cheek.

"What's waiting for you that's better than this?" Chad brushed his lips over her forehead.

When she failed to respond, he grazed lower, inhaling her fragrance. Each touch of his lips was like a tiny shock. Sabina pulled her face away and buried it against his chest.

Chad looked down at the curving bell of hair which separated above the slender column of her neck. He bent forward to kiss her exposed nape.

He staggered backward as she threw her arms around his neck and pulled his mouth to hers and kissed him deeply.

It was Chad who broke the kiss. Not in his aunt's house. For the first time, Chad realized his Midwestern morality was alive and healthy.

His movement startled Sabina, and she moved from

his embrace. "I . . . I don't know what came over me. Let me go, Chad. Please."

Sabina freed herself and he reached for her, clasping her chin lightly. "Sweetheart, I don't know why you're apologizing. I've never been kissed like that before in my life."

She said seriously, "I *never* give in to impulse. In fact, I've never *had* an impulse like that."

Chad smoothed the worried frown from the smooth expanse of her forehead. "Then maybe it's time you did."

"There was something about the way you kissed my neck. Do you know no one ever did that before? Not even my fiancé."

An ingrained self-protective instinct made Chad pull away as he spoke. "Your *fiancé*?"

"Oh, not anymore. Not for over six years," Sabina said. "What if I'd said I was still engaged and that he was a bad-tempered professional football player?"

Chad threw his arm around her shoulder, drew her to his side, and led her into the cozy den. A hissing bed of embers played counterpoint to the moaning wind outside. "I'd have been hunting my passport and a plane ticket to Siberia. We have to talk." He sat her firmly at one end of the couch and placed himself at the other end, leaving the middle cushion to serve as chaperon. "There's nothing sinful about kissing. I've always enjoyed it."

"I don't know what came over me," Sabina said seriously, as if pondering her uncharacteristic behavior.

"I want to know more about you. This evening is the first time you've let out more than a peep about yourself. On the other hand, you probably know enough about me and my family to write a book." He slid the base of his spine to the edge of the couch, stretching his legs toward the fire. "You have a brother. Where did you grow up?"

Sabina's mind went blank. Then she stammered, "In . . . in Golden, Colorado."

"There, that was easy, wasn't it? Are your parents still there?"

"Yes."

"Where's your brother?"

"Jack's in Bangor, Maine." She smiled before adding, "We both moved far away. My parents don't seem to notice."

"Do you keep in touch?" Chad asked curiously. He spoke with his own parents in Phoenix several times a week. They picked up the telephone as casually as if they lived on opposite sides of town.

Sabina's voice was devoid of emotion. "Mother calls every month or six weeks. She and Dad are immersed in their careers. Neither of them writes letters." She knew he couldn't comprehend that kind of relationship. Would he believe she had never before thought it unnatural? "Jack and I keep up with each other. We've always been close," she added defensively.

Translation: You're all either of you have, Chad thought. No wonder she was so prickly and indepen-

dent. She'd never known anything different . . . unless
. . . "What about your ex-fiancé?"

She lifted both hands, running them through her hair
and lifting it above her head. The shining strands returned obediently to a smooth bell. She sighed. "I was
always idealistic. Causes and issues—like conserva-
tion—attracted me, maybe because we talked about
them at home.

"I made friends with people who felt the same way.
We protested . . . or whatever we felt had to be done.
John and I became good friends. After graduation, it
seemed logical to plan marriage, so we could continue
to make a difference. We were very idealistic," she
defended.

His gaze fixed on the ceiling, Chad nodded encour-
agingly. He supported numerous worthwhile causes,
and he had seen the zealous intensity of those who
lived their beliefs. Perhaps if he hadn't, at an early
age, accepted responsibility for the people who de-
pended upon him for their livelihood, he might have
been the same.

Sabina was grateful he wasn't looking at her. She
couldn't explain her broken engagement face to face.
"We used different approaches. He was an activist,
catching the public eye. I wanted to work within the
system. He was gone more and more, sometimes even
in jail. I . . . didn't even miss him." She swallowed
nervously. "There wasn't any magic." The sentence
flew from her lips before she could stop it.

Sabina glanced sideways to assure herself Chad was

still inspecting the ceiling for possible cracks. "In the end, I realized we wouldn't have much of a marriage."

There. She'd said it. Jack had never liked John, and had made no secret of his estimate of her intelligence for considering marrying such a loser. She risked another sideways glance.

His head propped in the wing of the couch, Chad was staring at her as if he'd never seen her before. It was several moments before he spoke, and when he did his voice was at the dangerously quiet level she'd heard the day before when he'd dissected Jonas for allowing her to drive the front-end loader.

"Let me get this straight. That wimp neglected you. He disappeared on little jaunts where he expended what little emotion he had on protests. I suppose when he came home he blamed you for anything that went wrong."

She glared at him. "I *did* figure out the problem before I did anything serious, like marry him! Not every family in the world is like yours. I'm not accustomed to people who really *care* about each other. They even seem to care about *me*."

"Why not? Is there something wrong with you? That selfish . . . He really did a number on you, didn't he?"

Where was the cool, analytical thinking she prided herself on? She couldn't admit he unsettled her so completely she was ready to bite her fingernails. "I'm here to inspect Calico, so I expected everyone to be distant. Instead, they treat me as if they've known me forever." She frowned. "I could get in big trouble for becoming involved with you. It might look as if one of us were trying to . . . to subvert the other.''

''The attraction between us is real. There's no reason we shouldn't see if there's something more, now that your inspection is finished.'' He reached for her hand, capturing it as she tried to pull away from him.

Sabina shrank into the pillows at her back. The more they talked, the more confused she became.

He remained where he was, his eyes alight with skepticism. ''You horrified poor Jonas yesterday when you showed up at the office. He watched you take off that 'city' coat and snap on your chains. Your efficiency gave him such a fright he called the site to hedge his bets. You switched gears on him too fast, but you're not too fast for me.''

''He called me 'Missy.' If he'd been younger I'd have punched out his lights.''

Chad's grin widened. ''Why didn't you do that to me when you realized I fudged on the weather report?''

''By the time I knew, I wasn't as eager to leave.'' She ducked, knowing he would lunge for her, then rolled beneath his arm and slid to the floor. ''That was a major mistake. I should have been on the road before you got here this morning.''

She didn't rise quickly enough. Chad levered himself off the couch in one fluid movement, landing next to her. His arm anchored her to the braided rug and he kissed her. She felt the solid thud of his heart.

The power of her response astonished her. His eyes, deep amber, dancing with deviltry, were inches from her own. Sabina couldn't look away. When his strong fingers finally threaded through her hair to cup the back of her head, he whispered softly, "Don't look so scared. I haven't done anything yet."

"So the man says," she murmured before he kissed her again.

"Smile for me."

Confused, she stared at him blankly.

"I said smile. Please?"

Sabina smiled.

"That sneaky dimple of yours is . . ."

"*Woof!*"

The sound brought Sabina back to reality. Sock advanced several paces into the room to repeat his demand. There was no doubt of his need.

Chad groaned and rested his forehead briefly against Sabina's shoulder before raising his head and looking ruefully into Sabina's eyes. "He wants out. Now. I know that bark."

Sabina looked at Chad's tousled hair glinting gold in the dying firelight. Regret, mixed with near-relief at the interruption, filled her. "You'd better let him out. I . . . should turn in."

He stood, holding out his hand to help her to her feet. "Maybe you'd better. Sleep well. I'll see you in the morning."

"Time to rise, Sunshine!"

Chad chuckled as Sabina growled and burrowed more deeply beneath the fat comforter. He stared at the motionless mound on the bed, weighing several options. Then he acted.

Sabina shrieked as the comforter disappeared. "Get out of here!"

"I could have wakened you with a kiss, like the prince in *Sleeping Beauty*." Righteousness was not a role Chad wore well.

"Maybe you should go bury yourself in a snowbank."

"The sun's been up for three hours, and so has the temperature. Those snowbanks are already shrinking."

"So go play in one before it melts," Sabina said reasonably.

"You really are testy in the morning, aren't you?" Chad wrapped the comforter around her shoulders. "Do you cross-country?"

"My track shoes are at home," she grumped.

"Ski, my sweet."

She nodded irritably, her eyes still closed.

"You shouldn't frown like that. Causes wrinkles," he warned. "I dug out skis and a set of boots that should fit you. If you hurry, we can get out before the snow melts."

"You woke me for that?"

"We don't have a lot of big-time treats available for you city girls. Of course, if you're out of shape, we won't bother."

Sabina pulled the cover closer around her shoulders and curled into a ball. "Wake me when the roads are clear."

"Suit yourself, but Aunt Clara's making eggs Benedict."

She heard him leave as she pulled the covers over her head. She counted to ten. His dig about her physical condition rankled. She'd show him a thing or two about cross-country skiing. Besides, she would kill for eggs Benedict. Sabina crawled from her warm nest and staggered to the shower.

Twenty minutes later, she glowered at Chad as he greeted her with a bowl of fresh fruit in one hand and a steaming coffee mug in the other.

"You two must have had quite an evening if you're still tired after sleeping this late," Erica commented cheerfully.

Sabina nearly choked on a piece of pineapple.

"I never heard you come upstairs, Chad," Clara commented.

"I was out with Sock. He didn't want to come in."

Eyeing her nephew, Clara observed, "I 'spect you both needed a snowdrift to roll in."

"You may be right, Aunt Clara," Chad responded sunnily.

Sabina was becoming accustomed to hearing virtual strangers discuss her private life in her presence. She just couldn't get angry with Clara. When she left here she would miss her and the twins . . . and Chad.

The realization was like a physical blow. Talking about her past with Chad had made her realize how restricted her life had been.

"Turning me down on the skiing?"

"I'm not out of condition," she parried.

"Good. Then you'll come. I waxed the skis just in case."

Sabina pretended reluctance, but she would never have turned him down. She wanted the memories.

In no time at all she was trudging alongside Chad through the heavy snow toward the edge of the little town.

"We can't ski till we cross the main drag. The plows have cleared it," Chad explained as they started out.

Sabina followed close behind him. In spite of her dark glasses, the bright March sunshine made her eyes water. Snow transformed the buildings into frosted gingerbread structures straight from *Hansel and Gretel*. The sun's laserlike rays reflected diamonds from the white landscape as far as she could see. "I can't believe this all happened in such a short time."

"Look your fill. The snow will disappear just as quickly. It's March." Chad helped her over a split-rail fence. "We can put on our skis now." He knelt to clean the slots on the soles of her boots before slipping the skis into place.

Moments later, she followed him across the rolling expanse of white, quickly remembering to coordinate the rhythm of poles and skis. Chad needed no such adjustment period, and he drew ahead effortlessly.

They flowed across the field until Chad gestured for her to stop at the top of a small rise. "This is as good a place as any to catch your breath. Listen to the quiet."

Total peace surrounded Sabina. She couldn't remember ever feeling so cut off from the world. She glanced over at Chad. Her voice low, she observed, "You do a lot of this."

Although his eyes were unreadable behind dark lenses, she saw his mouth tighten. "Those are Marie's skis and boots you're wearing. The three of us used to ski a lot. Now I get out whenever there's snow; it seems to bring them closer. Sometimes I come at night in the moonlight." He adjusted the strap of his pole. "Being out here reminds you you're not the center of the universe, that you can't control everything that happens."

Her throat tightened at the resignation in his voice.

"Zack and I were closer than most brothers. He's gone, but the sun still comes up every day. There are still surprises." His lips quirked irrepressibly. "Sometimes even a state inspection is serendipity." He looked across the field below them and pointed. "Follow me. I've something to show you."

Minutes later, flushed and exhilarated, Sabina glided to a stop at the edge of a ravine. The sound of rushing water drew her eyes, and she glanced downward at the icy stream already swollen by melting snow. "Can we get down there?"

"We'll have to take off our skis to get through the undergrowth."

She was releasing her bindings when Chad's shout startled her. As she straightened, she saw him slide down the steep slope on his back, grabbing for branches on either side of him as he hurtled toward the frigid water. Her heart pounding in her throat, she fumbled with the recalcitrant skis. Her hands shook even more than before, but they finally swung loose.

At the lip of the ravine, she peered down. He was sprawled, unmoving, against a large bush not three feet from the edge of the stream. She called his name, her voice echoing in the sparkling silence. Squelching panic, she grasped a sapling to keep from falling as Chad had, then reached ahead to another tree, shifting from tree trunks to shrubs and back to trees as she negotiated the steep incline. Fear for him made her blood pound so loudly in her ears she couldn't hear the rushing water below her.

Chad lay partially on his left side, his eyes closed. Sabina knelt beside him and reached for his wrist to check for a pulse, her lips forming his name over and over. Her skin felt dead and numb with fear. "Chad, talk to me."

His hand gripped her arm and her feet left the ground. For a moment, Sabina thought she would land in the freezing water, but she underrated Chad's control. A dexterous twist of his wrist turned her in mid-air. Chad's hands cushioned her descent.

The unexpected takedown held Sabina quiet long enough for Chad to murmur triumphantly, "I told you I'd surprise you."

"You faked this whole thing just to prove you could catch me unawares?" The little voice she usually obeyed demanded that she protest, but the voice had no sense of humor.

Chapter Nine

"This wards off frostbite. The tips of your ears were a little red," he whispered.

He pulled her head down and kissed her.

"Chad . . . ?" She leaned forward and kissed him back, then sighed, a small, disappointed sound. Sabina had a mental picture of the two of them lying in the snow while the icy stream burbled merrily alongside. Sanity returned, and she drew away from him. "This is *so* unprofessional. Until my report is filed, I'm here officially."

"What if I told you we'd crossed the county line and you were no longer near my place of operation?"

"I'd say you were trying to sell me Grant's Tomb."

Chad rose, drawing Sabina with him. With exaggerated precision, he tugged her wool hat over her ears and rested his forearms on her shoulders before lowering his forehead to hers. "This isn't over." His breathing was quick and light, his voice deadly serious. "We need time together. Away from my family, from our jobs."

Sabina nodded shakily.

"You *do* want to see me after you've finished your report, don't you?"

The question circled wildly in her thoughts. She felt like a teenager who'd been asked for her first date. "When?"

"It may take me a few weeks." His voice was pensive. "I wasn't looking for something as important as this to happen to me."

He tipped her chin upward, his coffee-colored gaze locking with hers. Bright sun lightened the bleached tips of his thick lashes and highlighted the lean plane of his cheek. "I think we can be very good for each other."

For the first time in her life, Sabina glimpsed a future filled with love. Her smile felt tremulous, and she knew her heart was in her eyes. "If you don't come, I'll track you down. I might even put out a warrant on you."

Chad flicked her cheek with his fingers. "I'll bank on that." He drew away. "We'd better go home before they send out a search party."

The return trek took no time at all. Exhilarated, Sabina threw herself into the rhythmic glide of her skis, staying close behind him, filled with a sense of euphoria. The sunlight flashing off the brilliant white landscape and the exercise made her giddy. She laughed aloud with pure joy.

As they approached the rear of the house, the door flew open to reveal Daniel's lanky figure. "Chickened out last night, didn't you, Chad? I'm pretty hurt."

Daniel's broad smile didn't indicate any permanent damage. Accepting their congratulations with aplomb, he stepped back to allow them entrance. "What were you doing? Making snow angels?'' The teenager brushed snow from Chad's back. As Sabina turned, he removed a dead leaf from the cuff of her hat. ''Oh ho! What have we here? Showed her the leaf slide, did you, Chad?''

Sabina stopped in mid step. ''The what?''

Erica joined them in the warm kitchen. ''It's sort of a gully down the side of a ravine, and the leaves collect in it. If there's snow, you don't need a sled or anything. You just throw yourself on your back and go whoosh!''

Sabina felt the color rise in her cheeks. She turned toward Chad, who was making rather a project of opening the refrigerator door. Unreasonably, she felt like the odd man out—the child who hadn't been let in on the joke.

Oblivious to her distress, Daniel reached out to brush snow off her shoulder and teased, ''Fooled you, did he? Bet you rushed to the rescue.'' He waggled his eyebrows teasingly.

Sabina fled. In her haste to push through the swinging door, she nearly struck her hostess in the face with the heavy panel. Remorse made her stop to apologize, but Clara demanded, ''Did that nephew of mine play that old leaf slide trick?''

Sabina couldn't respond. Lovely as it had been to feel part of that great, warm circle of concern, she felt as if she were expected to enjoy having the details of her love life under general discussion. She felt her lips tremble and heard the thinness of her own voice as she said, "Since Daniel's home, I assume the roads are passable. I really should be on my way."

She rushed into the little apartment before Clara could answer, missing the determination on the face of the older woman.

Pulling off the knit hat, Sabina resisted the impulse to stomp on it and settled for hurling the thing onto the couch. Her parka followed. She reached into her closet for her dress boots and coat, determined to make her exit with all the dignity she could scrape together.

Her parents might be cold, but at least they gave a person privacy. The openness which had seemed so endearing had lost its appeal. She was a grown woman, and she didn't need a pair of precocious twins doing a running commentary. She told herself she'd been right in her assessment the day before—get out of town and run as fast as you can.

The zipper on her boot jammed, and she jerked furiously at the tab, breaking a fingernail. Forcing herself to slow down, she freed the zipper and fumbled in her handbag for an emery board.

The nail smoothed and her coat wrapped around her like armor, she closed the panel behind her, determined to escape before anyone asked any more embarrassing questions.

An uneasy silence pervaded the kitchen as, carrying her luggage, she backed through the swinging door. Daniel made a halfhearted move to rise from his chair to help her, then sank back down at a quick motion of Chad's hand. Clara stepped forward from her position at the stove.

"No need for you to rush off, Sabina. Daniel and Erica won't pry no more." Her glance stabbed at the pair, as if to reinforce a lecture already delivered. "I'd like it real well if you'd stay the weekend."

Ignoring Chad as if he were invisible, Sabina managed a polite smile. "I really must get back. I'm already a day overdue. Besides, you know what they say about fish and guests. After three days, they start to smell funny."

The elderly woman leaned forward abruptly and kissed her cheek. "It's been real nice to have you. Come back."

Disarmed by the affectionate gesture, Sabina allowed Chad to remove her clothing bag and carryall from her hands and disappear through the outer door. Embarrassment at her childish reaction was fast replacing the anger she knew was unreasonable, but search as she could, the proper words wouldn't spring to her tongue. Instead she murmured, "Thank you. You've been wonderful."

The twins' subdued farewells followed her through the door. She dreaded another encounter with Chad. She wanted to leave and get it over with. The realization that she had just behaved unreasonably far overbalanced her imagined humiliation at being one of a series of women romanced in that wooded hollow.

Chad watched Sabina stride briskly away to her car. Her movements and her "city" clothes distanced her from him. There was no way he could take back his cousins' teasing. Didn't she know it stemmed from affection, that they expected her to laugh with them? They'd paid her a compliment, but he knew she hadn't seen it that way. She needed more time to adjust to the free and easy give-and-take of his outspoken family.

Watching her firm jaw and the proud set of her head, Chad swore to himself that if he had the opportunity to surround Sabina Hanlon with love, nothing would ever make her unhappy again.

His thoughts shook him down to his ski boots.

The car door slammed sharply; she rolled down the window and said, "I'll send you a copy of my report. As you already know, your operation is clean and progressive. I appreciate your cooperation."

To his sensitive ears, the stilted phrases sounded forlorn. Chad leaned toward the window. "You haven't seen the last of me. I'm coming after you. Maybe when you're on your own turf you'll acknowledge what's possible between us. And you won't care who knows it." Ducking his head inside the open window, he kissed her. Hard.

"Incidentally, the last time I tricked a girl down the leaf slide I was a senior in high school."

To his surprise, her eyes sheened with moisture and a piteous expression twisted her mouth before she said softly, "The last time I let myself overreact so rudely, I was in kindergarten."

Two weeks had passed. Two weeks during which Sabina had alternated between beating herself over the head for her childish behavior and yearning for Chad's presence. After the first night, spent chafing at the pitfalls of conducting a fledgling romance with a Greek chorus in the background, she had realized that for the first time in her life she felt alive. How odd that she hadn't been aware of her stultified condition.

Her senses were now attuned to everything. Early April's promise of spring made her feel giddy and free. Her cheeks warmed and her pulse rate rose at the thought of Chad, and she welcomed the feelings, wallowing in anticipation.

In retrospect, the trip to Calico Mining replayed as a *Brigadoon*-like interlude, but Sabina had no intention of waiting a hundred years for Chad.

Any anger inside her bubble of well-being was directed toward herself for the years of human warmth she'd missed. As each day had passed with no word, the new Sabina toyed with the idea of staging a surprise inspection at Calico, then discarded the idea as unprofessional.

Her thoughts retraced familiar ground as she stirred tomato sauce. Her hand slipped, and the thick red mixture splashed upward. Ignoring the stain on her shirt, she dabbed at her cheek with a paper towel. The sound of the doorbell interrupted her efforts. If it was a salesman calling on a Saturday evening, she intended to send him home with an earful.

The figure lounging at her door seemed larger than life. Had she caused Chad to materialize just by thinking of him? There he stood, looking even more wonderful than she remembered. She yearned to be cool and sophisticated, but her brain wouldn't relay the message to her lips. Instead she said, "It took you long enough."

Sabina didn't even smile to take the edge from her words.

He asked quizzically, "I don't want to seem critical, but have you fallen into a vat of spaghetti sauce?"

Sabina cast a horrified look at herself. The dollop which had struck her minutes earlier hadn't been the first to splatter the front of her oversize shirt. She wondered where else the stuff had landed. "I'm making lasagna."

"Shall we just go on standing here and looking at each other, or may I come in?"

Sabina stepped back so he could enter.

Chad removed her fingers from the door and closed it behind them. He leaned forward and licked a spot of sauce from her cheek, then held her face between his warm hands as he kissed the tip of her nose. "Delicious. I can hardly wait to see your kitchen," he teased.

In an effort to still her racing pulse, she moved away from him and said dryly, "You're making yourself right at home for someone who took his time getting here."

"You didn't exactly issue a warm invitation when you took off in such a rush," he reminded her. "I decided to come anyway."

Memory of her hurried departure opened a wound in her conscience. "I tried to apologize when I wrote your aunt a bread-and-butter note, but things were so hard to explain. . . ." *Impossible,* she thought. She'd been accepted into their family circle without question, but she had still felt alien. She'd wanted only to crawl back to her apartment and draw the door in behind her. Time and distance had given her perspective.

"My love life fascinates Aunt Clara and the twins, mostly because they've never been able to find out enough. I never date anyone local, which drives them wild. My reputation is mostly a figment of their imaginations, and they know it. Then you came." There was no resentment in his voice, only fond laughter.

"They love you very much."

"I know. That's why I try to make them happy by gingering things up now and then. Gives them more to speculate about."

Chad made a sudden resolution. After her response to him two weeks earlier, she had rushed off as if the dogs were after her. He wanted her to open her mind and her heart to him—and to his family, which had already taken her in, whether she knew it or not. He kept his voice steady as he said, "We're going to start from scratch. As if I'd never kissed you and you'd never responded to me. Please, Sabina?"

Sabina flashed the dimple that intrigued him and turned toward the kitchen. "I have to finish my lasagna. Would you like something to eat?"

"I wouldn't turn it down," he said. The offer relieved any fears he had that she might send him packing.

"Then follow me," she said.

His suspicion that her entire kitchen would be spattered with tomato sauce was unfounded. On the glass table where she seated him were half a dozen single-serving containers already filled with lasagna and thickly sprinkled with shaved mozzarella cheese. She popped one into the microwave.

Without speaking, she gestured him to a chair and set a place for him. When the oven announced the completion of its time, she returned to the task of wrapping the remainder in plastic film and zipping them in plastic freezer bags before crowding them in around a variety of ice-cream containers. "I haven't room for all this unless we eat the ice cream. Strawberries 'n Cream?"

Chad thought the flavor perfectly described the becoming rose flush high on her creamy cheeks. Sabina was offering to meet him halfway. "My favorite," he replied softly.

Sabina had always considered her kitchen spacious. With Chad lounging in the captain's chair, the room's dimensions shrank to those of a closet. Fresh air blended with the fragrance of the tomato sauce, creating a homey atmosphere, but Chad's presence added something she'd never realized she craved. The discovery panicked her, and she searched her mind frantically for a safe conversational topic. "How are the twins?"

"Daniel's coming out of his depression after the team lost in the finals, and Erica has dress rehearsals for the play this week." Chad's voice was amused, and his gaze was focused on the lasagna-laden fork in his left hand. He continued, "Aunt Clara is in the thick of the infighting at her church circle over the spring mother-daughter banquet. Some lazy types want to downgrade the event to an evening dessert gathering, and she's on her horse. Jonas is the same as ever, only furious because the crew voted to call our encounter a draw and all the bets were returned.''

His eyes twinkled when he finally looked at her. ''And that's all the news I have. Can we start the getting acquainted phase of our courting now?''

Sabina dropped the half-gallon ice-cream container she'd been holding into the sink and began to laugh. ''This is never going to work,'' she finally managed. ''We don't have a thing in common.''

He was at her side before she could move, pulling the ice-cream scoop from her hand and competently filling the glass bowls she'd set out. ''That's why I'm here. Do you like sports?''

''Of course.'' She accepted the bowl he placed in her hands and dug in the drawer beside her for spoons.

''There's no 'of course' about it. Since we're baring our souls, I'll let you in on a secret. My R and Rs that the twins make so much of are actually trips to Cavalier and Indian games. And someday, when the Browns are back, I'll have a football team to follow again.'' The laughter lines at the corners of his eyes deepened. ''The whole town thinks I slip away and party, and if you ever tell anyone otherwise, I'll have to hurt you badly.'' He took his own bowl to the table and sat down.

Ignoring the laughing threat, Sabina settled herself across from him. ''You're a fake.''

"Harmless fun. Since I'm still single, Aunt Clara enjoys painting me as just a little profligate. I suspect she knows better, but it sure doesn't hurt her stock around town. Didn't you know small communities thrive on the idea of a little sin touching them?"

"I think you're trying to sell me a bag of moonshine," she answered, digging her spoon into the ice cream.

"Nope. I'm trying to sell you me. I don't gamble, except for a monthly low-stakes poker game with a few old friends. I don't drink to excess, and I'm kind to widows and orphans." He smiled at her winningly and said coaxingly, "Mothers love me."

Her laughter fled, and Sabina looked at him. Really looked at him. His eyes were as clear and sincere as a solemn baby's. The man was serious. "This has gotten out of hand."

Chad reached over and patted her hand. "Nothing would make me happier. Now, what about you? I know you have a secret addiction to slinky underclothes. Aunt Clara still hasn't recovered from that thing you were wearing the day Sock bushwhacked you. Any other hidden vices I'm going to have to adjust to?"

Sabina thought she might be going mad, but she was so charmed she went along with the game. "I live a very boring, squeaky-clean life. My only vice is shooting the occasional mine operator who offends me." Sure that would throw him a roadblock, she determinedly scooped a spoonful of ice cream into her mouth.

"I'd already heard about that through the grapevine," he said cheerfully. "What do you do in your spare time?"

"Cook," she answered, waving an explanatory hand toward the stove. "I work long hours, and I hate junk food, so my freezer is well stocked with homemade microwave dinners."

"What else?"

"I read and swim laps at the Y when I'm in town."

"And . . ."

"That's it," she said helplessly. "I'd like to travel to Mexico someday. The mountains there have some great rock formations to explore."

Chad scraped his bowl and shook his head disapprovingly. "You don't know how to really relax, Deputy Inspector. Have you been to a concert at the Ohio theater, to Schmidt's for bratwurst and German music, or to the Columbus Zoo? Or more to the point, to The Wilds, which isn't that awfully far from Calico?"

"I've been here less than a year. And I hate zoos. Animals shouldn't be penned up and put on display," she said defensively.

"Let's see. I'll bet you've ignored The Wilds because you don't want to admit someone could conceive of anything so creative as a wild animal preserve on reclaimed land. You should give thanks I've come to broaden your outlook, Sabina." He stood and looked at his watch, then set his bowl in the sink and filled it with water. "Be ready by nine-thirty tomorrow morning. I'm going to take you around town and show you what you've been missing."

His assumption that she would drop everything at his demand irritated Sabina, and she rose from her chair and faced him across the kitchen. "What makes you think I'll change my plans just to racket around town tomorrow?"

Chad rounded the table and kissed her fleetingly. "You just admitted you don't do anything but work and cook. You cooked tonight, and tomorrow's a play day. Be ready." With that he was gone.

Chapter Ten

Chad looked around as he pushed the button at Sabina's door. Dew sprinkled on the grass in the courtyard outside Sabina's apartment. The sprawling, one-floor plan buildings looked as if the management crew had just painted all the woodwork. Fresh mulch surrounded each small shrub, and he knew without asking that geraniums would be planted within a month, probably exactly eight inches apart. The very perfection of the little complex made him sigh. Sabina had selected an apartment that matched her upbringing—sterile and perfect. He had his work cut out for him.

Still, he had no complaints about her prompt response to his ring. Nor about her appearance. The lady inspector looked good enough to eat in her crisp khaki slacks and pale pink cotton sweater. Before she could say a word, he leaned forward and kissed her heartily. "I love a prompt woman," he said as he drew back.

"I . . . Chad, you said we were starting from the beginning. I can't think clearly when you kiss me like that."

"Good. That means I'm getting to you," he said as he led her to his car. He liked her confusion. The poor

138

thing had to learn how to separate her job from her personal life. "Have you been to Crater's yet? Their omelettes are famous."

"I'm too cranky in the morning to go out to eat."

"That's a thing of the past." The discovery that Sabina hadn't bothered to explore the city for its hidden treasures appalled him. She focused all her energies on her work, never noticing the everyday pleasures that make life an adventure. Chad felt poetic, thinking of her as a bud that was just now blooming . . . and of himself as the master gardener.

She'd quickly masked her wistfulness when confronted with his plain-speaking, loving family, but on several occasions he'd seen her confusion give way to flashes of poignant envy. The world in all its infinite variety was out there, and he would show it to her. He felt as if he were about to take a child to the circus for the first time.

He knew his smile was beatific, even as he searched for a parking spot in the narrow German Village streets. Today he would knock himself out to expose Sabina to the world of simple, unthreatening relaxation.

"I've never seen anyone so happy about having to park half a mile from a restaurant," Sabina teased, as, hand in hand, they walked along the brick sidewalk.

The breeze worried at the edges of her light jacket, the sun warmed her shoulders, and Chad treasured the way she was getting into the spirit of the morning. He watched each person they passed responding to her happiness. She'd already given in to his scheme to simply fritter away a day spontaneously.

"After breakfast, tell me if it was worth it."

"The food can't be any better than your aunt's."

"No, but every bit as good." He tugged her hand. "This is a necessity—a serious breakfast to start the day and fuel the body so we can do some serious time-wasting."

He remembered sitting next to her at the maple table in Clara Kincaid's kitchen, scarcely conscious of the food he ate because of his awareness of her. This morning was even better. He had her all to himself.

"You look like a little girl on her first merry-go-round ride." The glowing pleasure on her face humbled Chad. For one swift moment, he experienced fear that he might inadvertently let her down. Fear was an unfamiliar emotion to him. He was accustomed to caring for others; he'd been raised with a sense of duty as natural as breathing. But that was different from making himself accountable for the happiness of someone he had suddenly realized was the most important person in his world. "Too bad there isn't a circus in town. I'd take you."

Sabina wrinkled her nose in distaste. "I hate the circus. The thought of those poor animals being dragged from place to place in cages, and never having any freedom makes me cry."

"You'll like the zoo. That's a promise."

"I'll try," she responded.

Chad tucked bills beneath his plate and picked up the check. "There are two sides to lots of things." His quick grin removed any sting from his words. He reached for her hand. "Come on. Let's go look at the baby gorillas. The only way they'll survive is in captivity."

In spite of her reservations, Sabina approved of the natural surroundings for the Columbus Zoo's famous gorillas. She had to be dragged away for lunch at the French Market.

She even enjoyed the Center for Science and Industry, but she realized by mid afternoon that she didn't want to share Chad with wild animals or Campfire Girls on a field trip. His constant casual touches, and their rapid discovery of each other's likes and dislikes as they made their way through the displays, made her feel alive. For the first time in her life, she felt like a desirable, functioning woman.

"Look at that lace gown," she exclaimed as they wandered by the displays of life in the past. "Peoples' lives were so different then. Corsets must have restricted women's activities something awful."

Chad grinned back at her. "Kept them helpless and at home."

Sabina made a face at him. "You'd have liked that. I thought all the chauvinists had been put in their place until I met you," she teased.

"I prefer to think of my attitudes as chivalrous," he protested.

"You sure didn't sound very chivalrous that day at the mine site."

Suddenly serious, he said, "I admit I might have

overreacted. After what the twins have been through, I realize I instinctively want to keep them under a glass dome. Remember, I didn't know about your experience. But then, you should be more aware than anyone that the cuts can be dangerous, even for someone who earns his or her living there.''

Sabina knew his fears were legitimate, but her heart ached for Erica and her dreams. Instead, she asked, ''Does that mean you won't take me down into the simulated coal mine the brochure mentions?''

''Down there in the dark? That's an even worse place for a tender morsel like you. Do you really want to see it?''

''Actually, I might get the teensiest bit claustrophobic, even though I know it's just pretend.'' She looked at her watch. ''Besides, we won't have time. The center closes in twenty minutes.'' Where had the day gone?

''I'd better get you home,'' he said, throwing his arm around her shoulders. ''I'd take you out to dinner, but I have to get back. A desk full of papers is waiting for me to go through before I can hit the sack tonight.''

They made their way out of the building and into the parking lot, where Chad had left his Jaguar. Sabina stopped several feet from the car and looked at it, shaking her head. ''Conspicuous consumption, Chad. If I had money in your bank, I'd run to check my balance.''

He unlocked the door and she stepped in, still teasing him about his car. As he joined her in the cozy interior, he said, "I earned this car the hard way, Ms. Inspector. Don't ask me to apologize for enjoying it."

Seconds later, emitting a well-bred snarl, the Jaguar prowled the emptying downtown streets.

"You'll get a ticket."

"You work for the state. Flash your badge," he shot back.

Sabina's giggles filled the car. She couldn't remember ever feeling so lighthearted. No one had ever told her she could talk nonsense with a man and fall in love at the same time. The realization shocked her, and her laughter faded.

"What have you been thinking about all this time?"

With a start, she realized they had come to a stop at her apartment entrance. She must have lapsed into a near coma for the past twenty minutes. Could she be in love with him after such a short time?

Would an honest answer make him feel trapped? He'd liberated her from a life devoid of human commitment. Causes were important, but they made unsatisfactory bedfellows. Chad made her feel wanted, cherished, and beautiful. She found herself wanting to give more and more in return. If this weren't love . . . Without stopping to think, she looked him in the eye and said honestly, "I'm examining the reasons why I think I'm falling in love with you."

Chad ran a not-too-steady finger across the shadowed vein beneath the thin skin of her temple. "I hope they're all good ones."

"It's an impressive list, but I still don't really know you."

"As in . . ."

"You work hard. You give your family and your work more attention and caring than I've ever seen." She frowned as she considered her next words. "But you were raised that way. What else do you believe in?"

"Mothers, apple pie, and the flag."

"I don't suspect anything awful, Chad. I'm just curious."

"Well, I can hardly go out and picket against surface mining or demand that banks donate all their profits to the poor, can I?" He shifted against the leather of the seat until he was leaning against the door. His eyes were wide and candid. "Love, I work for every charity and cause in the community where I live. I see to the welfare of my immediate family, not to mention that of shirttail relations from here to eternity. I try to keep two businesses as ethical and profitable as possible." He sighed.

"There's such a thing as burnout. If I don't get away once in a while I become someone even *I* don't like very well. Should I apologize if I go to sports events with friends, spend a week in the woods away from a telephone, or occasionally enjoy the company of a female?"

Sabina ran both hands through her hair before smiling at him sheepishly. "I guess that's my problem. I've never taken R and R. There's always so much to do . . . and so few to do it."

He touched the tip of her nose. "There has to be a point where you step back and admit no one person can do it all. And once in a while you need a day like today. A day to just run out and enjoy yourself. And you have to dream something special for yourself. That's half the fun . . . seeing if you can make the dream come true.''

She brightened. ''I nearly forgot. I actually did that. I'm going to Chicago to see the Chicago Lyric Opera perform next month. And I'm going first class.''

''Sounds wild and extravagant. Just like something a person who spends her time trudging through mining sites might do,'' he answered lightly.

''Don't make fun of me. The trip is a special treat.''

''You aren't in the habit of indulging yourself, are you?'' Chad paused. ''I'll make you a bargain. You come to a Cleveland Cavaliers game with me next weekend, and I'll take you to Chicago . . . first class and no strings.''

Sabina drew back to look at him suspiciously. ''Why would you do that?''

''Because I want you to love pro basketball as much as I do. Because it makes me happy to make you happy. Because I'm glad you think you're falling in love with me.'' His gaze was bottomless and tender.

The incongruous reasons satisfied her. She had no response except to kiss him.

Chad knew that whatever sacrifice he might make to get away for those weekends would be worth it. Had it been fate or merely coincidence which had brought Sabina into his life? Whichever, he owed providence a tip of his hat and undying gratitude.

He drew back from her warmth. ''I'd better leave.

I have a ton of paperwork to get through tonight, and when I checked my voice mail, there were no fewer than three messages from Erica demanding I meet with her and Daniel.''

''Demanding?'' Sabina's eyes were on her hands as she fumbled for her linen tote bag on the floor of the car.

''Probably *begging* is a better term. Erica can get melodramatic at times. I'm never sure if the crisis is major or minor.'' He suspected the latter. There had been a determined note in Erica's voice, as if she had worked herself up to calling him, as if she dreaded the confrontation even as she requested the meeting. ''You *will* come with me next weekend, won't you?''

''What?'' Her voice cracked slightly and she seemed distracted.

''I said, you *will* come to the basketball game with me next weekend, won't you? We can leave for Cleveland early Saturday morning and come back Sunday. We'll stay with a college friend and his wife who live up there. You'll like them.''

''Of course I'll come. I just wonder if you'll be able to make the time to get away again so soon?''

''Sabina, if I can't be with you when I want to, I'll have to find a new line of work.'' He grinned at her. ''Maybe you could do a pop inspection about the middle of the week?''

''I think after the report I just filed, my boss might question my sanity. If everyone operated the way Calico does, I'd be out of a job. Besides, I'm already scheduled.'' A tiny frown crossed her forehead.

"Come work for me," he quipped. "You have experience in the industry. If I had someone I trusted to run Calico, I'd never even think of selling. You know everything but the marketing, and I could handle that. In a few years, Daniel will take over. Then we'll find another job for you."

Daniel hadn't yet told Chad about his scholarship. Why hadn't he? Then Sabina recalled that only a week had passed since the basketball team had lost in the state finals. Daniel probably needed the time to recover from disappointment over the loss.

She'd been silent too long; she had to say something. "Are you asking me to join the enemy?"

Chad looked at her steadily. His eyes were unreadable in the glow of the streetlight at the corner. "Am I the enemy, Sabina?"

The question was stupid. She'd known as soon as the words left her lips. With characteristic honesty, she met his gaze directly. "No." She smiled when the little lines around his mouth relaxed. "Have I been treating you like one?"

He pulled her close once again. "Sabina, this adversary thing. . . . We're not as far apart as it appears. I'd hoped you would have figured that out by now."

"I'm sorry, Chad. It's just that I'm a little unsure of myself." The bite of his fingers on her shoulder made her feel weak, and she leaned into him.

"Friday's a long ways off," he murmured.

Chad took the driveway to his home much more slowly than his usual breakneck pace, viewing the

A-frame with new eyes. He'd built it as a refuge. Less than two years after Zack's death, his own father had suffered a heart attack which made his retirement imperative. Since his mother's arthritis benefited from the Arizona climate, it was unlikely they would return to Ohio, except for brief visits. The responsibilities of the bank, the mining company, and the family were all his.

This place away from pleas for his attention and caring was as necessary as breathing. There were times when he couldn't face another problem, times when he craved peace. This hideaway was enough off the beaten path that people respected his wishes. His telephone was unlisted, and only his relatives and a few trusted employees were aware of the number.

Now he was thinking of bringing a wife into his domain. In a few short weeks, Sabina had become more necessary to him than breathing. Somehow he would overcome her aversion to surface mining. The coal was there under the ground, and someone was going to take it out. Wasn't it better that the mining be done by people who cared about the land?

He'd left Columbus reluctantly, deciding he would be unwise to rush Sabina's burgeoning feelings for him.

That evening, in the steaming warmth of his hot tub, Chad nursed his beer and wished Sabina were with him. An owl hooted nearby. Small nocturnal creatures made rustling sounds in the nearby woods as they pursued their lives. He wanted to share it all with Sabina. God willing, he would. Soon.

Several hours of paperwork awaited him in his spare bedroom, which he used as an at-home office. He sighed, unwilling to desert his fantasies. The messages on his answering machine echoed through his thoughts. The twins wanted a family conference. He wondered idly what *that* was all about.

Nothing was as urgent as his dreams of having Sabina where he could see her each day, permanently and irrevocably. She was what he needed, what he'd always need. He glanced at the digital clock on the control panel of the hot tub. It was too late to call her now. She was to leave at five in the morning for her next assignment.

Chad shrugged off his disappointment as he pulled himself from the soothing water. Who she was inspecting, and the results of that visit, were none of his business. There'd been an almost imperceptible tightening of the delicate skin around her mouth when she had referred to her plans.

The phone in his bedroom rang, shattering his peace. The answering machine took over, and Erica's voice sounded as he wrapped the towel around his hips. "Chad, I know you're there. Moogie saw your car heading toward your place over an hour ago. We've *got* to see you. . . ."

He punched the star button. "I'm here, Erica," he broke in. "Is something wrong?"

"Oh, good. I *hate* talking to a piece of tape. Chad, Daniel and I *have* to talk to you. We can't wait."

"I got all six messages. Is this an emergency?"

There was a moment of silence on the other end.

"We heard you were bargaining with a buyer for Calico."

The muscles at the back of his neck tightened. He sighed. "Just fishing, Erica. I want to hear what he has to say."

"Chad, you can't!"

"I'd never do anything without discussing it with you and Daniel." He passed his hand over his face. The euphoria of the past day seemed far in the past. "I just want the figures. This is your decision, and it always will be."

Apology replaced the panic in her voice. "I'm sorry, Chad. I . . . we shouldn't have leaped to the wrong conclusion. Anyway, we *still* have to talk."

"Okay, okay. But I can't sit down with you till late Friday. I have to sandwich a week of work around a banking conference in Pittsburgh Tuesday and Wednesday."

"Chad . . . we don't want to crowd your space." Erica sounded suddenly very young and vulnerable.

Compassion warred with the tension freezing the back of his neck. "Erica, I always have time for you and Daniel. I always will."

Chapter Eleven

Thoughts of Chad filled Sabina's mind as she set out in the predawn darkness the following morning. Who would have thought she could become so quickly accustomed to a man in her life? And not just any man. She'd chosen someone engaged in a practice she had always despised—but he made her heart quicken just by entering a room. Never before had her apartment felt empty—until Chad had left his imprint in the atmosphere.

Was he in love with her? He hadn't answered her own tentative admission, but he hadn't run in the other direction, either. There had been an aura of . . . She decided he had looked and acted relieved, as if he had crossed a hurdle. Perhaps, in spite of his teasing job offer, he still had reservations about her wholehearted dislike of the mining industry. She had them herself, but she had confidence in his attitudes, and his work reassured her.

Joy bubbled up inside her. Was it superstitious to feel that if she said the words out loud something might spoil her happiness? She announced loudly, "I'm in love with Chad Peters." A fatuous grin spread across her face as she exited the freeway to a county road. Saying the words had been easy. Now she had only to convince Chad.

Sabina wasn't looking forward to this inspection. Reclamation should be in progress on two separate sites by now, but she had a sinking feeling Wilbur McDonald hadn't made a single move toward restoring the land. And she knew for a certainty that his provisions for handling runoff at the site he was currently working would be inadequate.

In September, Sabina had outlined what had to be done. In return, she'd received a pat on the shoulder, accompanied by a politely veiled intimation that she'd be better off at home—with her knitting. She had smiled politely before returning to Columbus, knowing full well the man didn't take her seriously.

A quick mental comparison of the conditions she expected to find at her destination had the inevitable effect of reminding her of the superb reclamation work Chad and Calico Mining had accomplished. She still hated the ugly disruption of centuries-old sediment. Yet Chad had made a believable case for use of the land and the minerals beneath.

Was his job offer serious? She knew she could operate the company, and she would see him every day, learn to know him the way she yearned to. She remembered the longing in his eyes. Was she taking too much for granted?

Sighing regretfully, she accelerated around a curve. The smell of growing things and damp earth filled her with an unidentified yearning, a sense of something wonderful on the verge of happening.

Sabina pushed aside her daydreams. If she allowed herself to relive the weekend, she'd never be able to concentrate on the distasteful task ahead of her. A wry smile tightened her mouth as she reminded herself of her reputation.

Before the day was out, Sabina was grateful she'd prepared herself for the worst.

"I'm sick of you smart-aleck inspectors coming down here and interfering," Wilbur McDonald blustered.

Sabina fought to stay calm. "Mr. McDonald, the law spells out everything for you. A man with your experience should find it just as easy to do things right as to do them wrong."

"I'm right glad to hear you mention my experience, young lady. The people who wrote those laws haven't ever tried to dig coal and make a profit. Not with all those fool rules."

Wilbur McDonald was a burly man with a "Dunlap" waistline, his belly extending well over his belt. His skin was weathered, and a CAT hat perched on a shock of white hair long overdue for a haircut. He punctuated every other word with a stab of his cigar in Sabina's direction. She refused to back down.

"You didn't just hear about these laws yesterday, Mr. McDonald. The act was passed twenty years ago! When I was here before, I spelled out specific infractions. You haven't corrected one of them!" She paused to steady her voice. "And now you've opened a new section without waiting for permits. You knew you'd never get them, didn't you?''

"I can always get permits. My friends in the State Senate are a lot more powerful than *you* are. All I have to do is say the word, and you'll be out on the street without a job.'' He waved the cigar with more emphasis.

In her short career with the state, Sabina had never before recommended closing an operation. Even after she spelled out the probable total in fines, he remained defiant, bragging about important connections who would explain the facts of life to her.

Sabina estimated McDonald's age at somewhere around seventy. In all probability, he would never adjust to regulation of the industry. At the time he went into mining, anything that was easy, quick, and profitable was the standard. There were no teeth in what few regulations there were, and influence and bribery had been rampant. She didn't doubt McDonald's contacts in the legislature would attempt to find a compromise on his licensing. That wasn't her problem.

"I don't care if the *governor* is your *son*. I want this equipment out of here today! You'll receive official notification before the week is out. You're welcome to file a protest.'' The sights she saw in her two-day visit frayed Sabina's emotions, and she cried herself to sleep in the plastic surroundings of her room in the only motel available.

The raw, eroded sites stayed in her mind all the way back to Columbus. She'd gathered samples and documented everything necessary to back up her charges. Then she'd taken photographs. The pictures might be superfluous, but they were proof. Her memory needed no refreshing for her to complete the paperwork.

All that carried her through until Thursday was the memory of Chad, of the way his mouth quirked into a crooked smile, of basking in the warmth of his coffee-colored gaze.

She wanted desperately to hear his voice, and as she let herself into her apartment, she looked at the clock before running bathwater and liberally pouring in scented bath oil. Chad should be either at home or at Clara Kincaid's by eight. She would soak, defrost some lasagna in deference to the memories it triggered, then talk with him from the cozy comfort of her bed. The prospect nearly dispelled the bleakness of the past week.

The door chime was barely audible above the roar of the water tumbling into the tub. Grumbling, Sabina turned off the taps and pulled the sash of her terry robe snug. The bell sounded again as her belt twisted away from her fingers, and she called, "Keep your shirt on. I'll be there."

She opened the door as the chime rang a third time. Surprise flooded her, and she reached out her arms delightedly. "It must be thought transference. I was going to call you as soon as I finished my—" The anger in Chad's eyes and the white line around his lips stopped her in mid sentence. "What's wrong?"

"I'm coming in. Your neighbors aren't going to be interested in what I have to say."

Stepping back, she closed the door behind him and leaned against it for support. This anger was frightening, far different from his explosion that day at the mine site. Her leg muscles felt inadequate; she wasn't sure she could stand by herself. "What's wrong?"

He turned jerkily, without his usual fluid grace. His hands were knotted in the pockets of his jacket and his feet were set squarely, as if he were ready for a fight and was afraid he would lose his resolve.

"I thought you understood there had to be some compromises about mining." He drew a deep breath and exhaled, his nostrils flaring. "I guess I forgot your reputation as a hardnose. I couldn't believe the stories I'd heard were about *you*."

Sabina tightened her belt, as if to protect herself from something she didn't understand, something frightening. "Chad, I don't know what you're talking about."

"Do you know how many men you put out of work when you shut down Wilbur McDonald? Seventeen! That's seventeen families with no money coming in. There aren't *five* living-wage jobs available in Vinton County, much less seventeen. What are those people to do?"

If Chad had attacked her for any other reason, Sabina would have crumpled; her limited experience with love made her fragile. When he questioned her professional decision, one with no shades of gray, she couldn't back down.

"That's not my problem. The man has been thumbing his nose at the rules since long before I came here.

His workers all knew it, and they went along with him. His problem is, he thinks the rules don't apply to him because the county is a depressed area.''

''That's not true,'' Chad responded in the dangerous purr he'd used when cursing at Jonas and the workers who'd allowed Sabina to drive the front-end loader.

She felt no more intimidated than she had then. In fact, she lowered her own voice to the same icy level. ''That idiot committed every violation on the books. He's been warned . . . time and time again. After inspecting the two sites he abandoned, I cried myself to sleep. Even rats won't live there!''

''I can't believe that. Wilbur's worked that area for years, and I've never once seen anything he hasn't put back within the minimum of the requirements. I'll grant you he's no landscape artist, but he follows the rules.''

''You're wrong. You're just sticking up for him because you've known him forever. He thinks laws are for everyone but him, and he's always done as he pleased. He delights in flaunting his connections. Besides, I'm a woman. What do *I* know?'' Tears gathered behind her eyes. By sheer force of will, she contained them. She watched Chad closely. His expression said he knew he'd gone off half-cocked, but now that he had made his accusations, he didn't know how to back off. Perhaps he was aware his anger had roots in his own frustration with Sabina's attitude toward mining. Of course he would defend an industry he'd known all his life.

"You neglected to factor in the welfare of the area. You didn't grow up with those people."

"I gave him warnings, and I gave him plenty of time. What was I supposed to do? Correct the offenses myself?"

"He'd never allow that." Chad's voice was pensive, almost as if his thoughts were elsewhere. "Wilbur's accustomed to taking his own sweet time, but he gets there. Try to put yourself in his shoes. How do you think he felt, being shut down by a woman?"

Sabina seized on his last sentence. "Now you've come to the real heart of it. If I'd been a man, Wilbur wouldn't be so upset. Poor Wilbur!"

"I didn't mean . . ."

Sabina wanted to roll back time. If she could start the day over, maybe this argument wouldn't be taking place. Nothing made sense, but she had to try, even though she risked losing the happy future she'd glimpsed in his arms. "*You* probably could have talked him into minimal compliance. Everyone comes to you with their problems . . . except those closest to you. Daniel and Erica are about to give up their fondest dreams. All because you've been *good* to them."

"What are you talking about?"

"Go home and ask them, and take your chauvinism with you. I intend to give a lot of thought to figuring out why I was so stupid as to fall in love with you. You're . . ." Words failed her. She wanted him gone. She wanted to cry like a baby.

"Sabina, you're talking riddles. What do the twins have to do with this?"

Sabina knew she was being overemotional, but she also knew she was right. What Chad considered chivalry was really thinly veiled chauvinism. If he couldn't accept her for her strengths as well as her weaknesses, there could be no true relationship between them. Could he be made to see how right Erica was for Calico? Even though she was a woman? "I don't want to talk anymore, not now. See for yourself about McDonald, about the twins."

Reaching behind her, she opened the door.

She saw the frustration on Chad's features when he realized she was serious. "All right. I'm leaving."

As he stood on the threshold, he stared straight into her eyes, and her resolve almost weakened—it would be so easy to tell him she was sorry, that she hadn't meant the things she'd said. But she'd meant every word.

"Don't think this is the last you'll hear from me," he threw over his shoulder as he walked down the sidewalk.

For the next hour, Sabina sat at her computer listing every bit of information she wanted from her office files the next day. Organizing in detail helped her keep her personal loss at a distance. She'd done her job the way it should be done; before she finished, Chad Peters would find out just how professional she could be.

But when she sat on her couch that night cuddled into her favorite quilt, lists were the furthest thing from her mind. The ceramic shoe lamp she'd made at her first, and last, attempt at crafts, glowed from the low chest in the corner. Chad had laughed extrava-

gantly at her bright orange handiwork. And he'd understood. She'd made so few rebellious moves in her
life. The shoe stood for all the times she'd been too
inhibited to speak up.

Conventional, restrained, sensible Sabina's romance
hadn't even lasted a week. And she'd been foolish
enough to fall in love into the bargain. She might
never see him again, but she would make sure he discovered she had operated by the book. In the dark of
night, being right didn't seem to matter, but it would
tomorrow.

By noon the next day, Sabina had copied all the
material pertinent to Wilbur McDonald. So incensed
was she that she never stopped to question the ethics
of releasing the information to someone outside the
department. In spite of Chad's thick-headed attitude,
she knew he had too much integrity to be careless with
the contents of the tan envelope.

During lunch, she sent her package, assured same-
day delivery. All she wanted to do was burst into tears.

Chad's day was progressing no better. The arrival
of Sabina's concise list of McDonald's infractions interrupted his interrogation of Jonas concerning Erica's
activities at the mine site. Jonas's responses dismayed
him, even though the gnarled little man accepted full
responsibility for allowing the girl access to the area.

After he had ripped open the package, Chad wished
Jonas were elsewhere. As a rule, packets of papers
received a welcome comparable to the arrival of strep
throat. At his show of interest, Jonas nearly fell out of

his chair stretching to see the contents. Removing the packet from his desk, Chad sat back to read each page in detail. Chad knew Jonas was also awaiting more reaction to his revelations about Erica's involvement at the site. He let him wait. This was more important.

A sinking feeling invaded Chad's stomach as he read. He feared he had just made himself the most colossal idiot on the planet. Surely McDonald hadn't ignored all these warnings. Finishing the last page, he closed his eyes and leaned back in his chair. The little man on the other side of the desk looked chastened but curious. With sudden insight, Chad realized he'd been taking his unhappiness out on everyone around him. Raising both hands to his face, he rubbed his cheeks. "I'm sorry, Jonas."

Jonas relaxed visibly, the twinkle returning to his eyes. "You been havin' temper tantrums all day, son. Thought you'd growed out of 'em."

"This might be the one that actually teaches me a lesson. I really blew it."

"Nothin's forever 'cept death and taxes." The old man chuckled at his own use of the old bromide. "Anythin' else can be fixed. A person has to learn how to say 'I was wrong,' and you just did."

"I was never very good at that kind of thing. Besides, you're not the one who deserves the biggest apology, and I'm not sure that person is going to be receptive."

Rising, Jonas pushed his cap to the back of his head and scratched the creased skin of his forehead. "Depends on how much it means to ya."

Chad stared down at the papers. He shuffled and straightened the pile, then thumped the stack decisively against the polished surface of his desk and stood. "I'm going to be in Vinton County tomorrow, Jonas. Probably all day. Can you handle everything here?"

The old man's curiosity was obvious, but Chad had no intention of explaining his absence. His pride had taken enough of a beating.

"I'll be at Aunt Clara's for the rest of the day. If Merton calls, or if anyone wants me, tell them they'll have to wait till Monday."

When Chad arrived at his aunt's late that afternoon, Erica took the offensive as he walked in the door. "You aren't selling Calico, Chad. I won't let you."

Twenty-four hours earlier, he'd made a complete fool of himself with the woman he loved. Still licking his wounds, Chad now realized he was about to have a serious confrontation with Daniel and Erica. He could have described himself as *chastened* and not felt melodramatic. "So we won't sell Calico. I never knew the company meant this much to you."

"*Erica's* the one who wants Calico, Chad. And she's going to have it, because I want her to." Daniel's jaw was set. "I know my dad thought I would take over, but if he were still here he'd understand why I don't want to. I have a scholarship to art school."

Chad was past surprise. "Why didn't you tell me this before? Did you ever think how much happier we all would have been if you'd told me at the beginning? Am I that unapproachable?''

"It's not that! Mom and Dad always assumed Daniel would take over when he grew up, just because he's male. Then after they . . . Anyway, it seemed sort of sacrilegious to think of anything else. You've done so much for us!'' Erica paused, eyeing him closely. "You know we'd die before we'd hurt you, Chad.''

"I just couldn't bring up art school,'' Daniel chimed in. "I felt I was betraying my dad. But my heart would never be in Calico if it meant giving up art.''

Erica added, ''I know I shouldn't have been sneaking out to the site, but I can't stay away.''

Chad wondered how he'd missed noticing her interest. Erica's enthusiasm should have been obvious to him. Sabina knew. Had she guessed? Or had the twins confided in her? "There's no reason you can't run Calico, Erica.''

She hugged him exuberantly. "I'm so excited. Sabina said if I told you how much it meant to me, you'd understand.''

The twins had opened their hearts to Sabina, while keeping him in the dark all this time. Chad wondered what else he'd missed.

"Chad, I can get my training at Ohio State. Then I could come home on the weekends to help out. Just in case you find a life of your own.'' She winked as she added the rider.

Her not so subtle suggestion touched a nerve, but he answered agreeably. "Of course. But don't kid yourself that you'll want to leave campus on weekends, Erica." He managed a teasing grin. "I expect there'll be guys around who are taller than you are. Your social life will blossom."

She burst out, "Chad, I want to help *you* for a change."

"I've always had everything I wanted. With you two away from home, I'll probably find myself looking for things to do." He forced a smile. For the first time in his life, he wanted to wallow in martyrdom.

Unaware of Chad's bleak thoughts, Daniel teased, "Maybe now you'll have more time to . . . you know, meet someone. Or maybe you already have."

"Contrary to public opinion, I haven't made great sacrifices for you two." As he said the words, he knew they were true. His love for them had been behind everything he'd ever done for the pair he loved so much.

Daniel continued, "Have you heard anything from Sabina lately? Ouch!" He turned to his sister. "Why'd you kick me?"

"I didn't kick you. I stumbled, and my shoe bumped your ankle. I'm *sorry*. I didn't know you were such a wimp."

Their exchange failed to bring Chad out of his depressed mood. He wished they'd stop asking for answers he couldn't give. For the first time, he understood why Sabina had been so uncomfortable with his family's openness.

"I'm going to go help Gran fix supper. She's in there cooking like crazy because we're all here to eat at the same time." As Erica left, she narrowed her eyes warningly at Daniel.

Chad wondered how much his aunt had guessed, and how much she'd tell Erica. He'd blundered on a large scale, and there was no way his family would allow him to lick his wounds in private.

Daniel had been incredibly clumsy, but then so had Erica, with her blatant change of subject. She'd always been the more intuitive of the pair, and he was almost relieved she was in the kitchen, probably pumping her grandmother for all she was worth. He reconciled himself to having his sins dredged out for family discussion.

Tomorrow he'd see the proof of his idiocy. If Sabina was right, and the way things were going she probably was, he knew what he'd find. She'd learned more about Daniel and Erica in three days than they'd confided in him during a lifetime. It stood to reason she'd discovered things he'd never known about Wilbur's operation.

Chad wondered if he could admit his blindness to her and expect her to love him in spite of it. Replaying in his mind the scene in her apartment, Chad wasn't sure an ordinary apology would help. He'd been brutal.

She was even on target with her accusation of chauvinism. Would she accept his attitude as one that still prevailed in some parts of the country that could be ten years behind the rest of the world in political correctness? His attitudes were already changing. There had to be some way to convince her he was trying—

some way other than crawling to her and apologizing. But if he had to, he would.

"Are you going to be around this weekend, Chad?"

"I'm checking out a mining operation tomorrow."

"Thinking of buying it?"

Was Daniel's suggestion the result of divine intervention? Sabina had said she'd cried after seeing the obscenities Wilbur had abandoned. The germ of an idea exploded in his mind. It was so perfect, his depression vanished.

"You know, Daniel, that's not a bad idea. If we're to keep Calico, I'll need to look for a manager soon. The bank needs more time than I've been giving. If we owned two small operations, it would be worthwhile to hire someone. Are you sure you don't want to come into the family business? Vision like that can't be taught."

Horrified panic crossed Daniel's open features. "Gosh, no. I mean . . . you did say you were impressed by my scholarship."

"I meant that, Daniel. And I'm so proud of you. I'm just sorry you had to feel guilty, instead of being able to celebrate."

The teenager clambered to his feet as if anxious to leave before Chad changed his mind. "I've got to call Angie to let her know everything's okay." He disappeared through the arch, leaving Chad alone in the comfortable den.

For the first time in two days, Chad felt a glimmer of optimism. His cousin's suggestion gave him a direction, one that might reestablish him in Sabina's eyes. The idea wasn't a bad business move, either. The only drawback was the time he needed to get things in place.

Chapter Twelve

Three weeks of sleeplessness had deteriorated Sabina's driving skills. After discovering herself on the berm for the third time in ten minutes, she realized she was nearly asleep at the wheel. A sign ahead advertised HOME COOKING, and in spite of past experience with the hopeful words, she pulled into the gravel parking lot. At least the building looked clean.

She needed quick energy. "A hot fudge sundae and black coffee, please," she told the waitress. Two other tables were occupied, one by a suited man filling in blanks on what looked like a call report, the other by two men wearing flannel shirts and billed hats.

The thumps of the coffee mug and footed glass dish on the counter drew her away from her inspection of the other customers. "Here you go," the girl announced with enthusiasm. Free for a moment, the waitress crossed the room to join the two men. "What's new, guys?"

"Not much, Tammy. Not much at all. I ain't in jail, so something must be right. Still got my job, too."

The other worker laughed heartily. "Just be glad you're not workin' for Calico. I hear some honcho from Spain's buyin' it."

"I don't hold with all these foreigners comin' in. Some Japanese guy bought out Jimmy Gilbert last month. At least no one got fired, but that still ain't good." He removed his cap and settled it more squarely on his head.

"The foreign guys tip real good," said the waitress.

Junior laughed again. "Sure. Then they take their profits home with 'em. Can't figure why Chad's thinkin' a' sellin'. They done real good last year. 'Sides, it ain't really his."

Sabina realized she was only twenty miles from Chad. She'd been at a site near the Pennsylvania border, and had lost track of her location. Hearing the familiar names gave her a pang. Poor Erica. Chad must have refused to give her a chance.

"No, but what he says pretty much goes. Sorry to hear it. Calico's a sweet little outfit." The waitress got a dreamy look on her face as she spoke.

"Think Chad'll hang around here more if he sells, Tammy?"

The girl rose, laughing. "Don't I wish! Sellin' out won't change that any."

"I hear he had a set-to with the state inspector some time back," the first speaker interjected. "The fellas had to cancel their bets. Seems no one could figure out if the Tough Broad left because Chad sent her off or because they argued to a draw."

Mention of the wagers sent Sabina toward the cash register remembering the old saying about eavesdroppers hearing nothing to their credit.

The conversation haunted her during the rest of the

trip to her home office, where Nancy, the receptionist, teased her about coming in at closing time. "What's the matter, don't you have a home?"

"I'm just in no hurry to get there. Spring always makes me a little blue," she said, realizing she'd spoken the truth.

"Come shopping with me tonight. Marshall Field's is having a sale, which is enough to cheer up *anybody*. That lacy underwear you like is marked down. Something new and daring should lift your spirits." Nancy winked broadly.

The receptionist was one of the few women friends Sabina had made in Columbus. They shared a love for swimming, and occasionally met at the health club to turn their weekly laps into races. "Sounds good. I'll be ready in a few minutes." She crossed the room toward the cubicle which afforded her a minimum of privacy.

Nancy's voice followed her. "News flash on one of your favorites, Sabina. McDonald called this morning to hustle the rest of the paperwork. He's selling out as soon as he knows the bottom line on his fines."

"Who'd buy *that* mess!" Sabina stopped dead in the middle of the large communal room.

Nancy fumbled through the files on her desk. "The guy you did last March. Here it is. Chad Peters." She waved the folder triumphantly.

"But he's selling Calico."

"Maybe he's moving."

Sabina's head whirled. Why was he doing this? She'd just spent three weeks trying to convince herself she hated him. The jobless men. That must be why.

Chad's purchase would, in the end, be not only charitable, but extremely profitable. If the deal included all the mineral rights McDonald had contracted, future profits would more than cover the reclamation. Chad must have discovered she was justified in what she'd done. *So why haven't I heard from him?* she asked herself.

Sighing, she leaned back in her chair. Telling Chad she was falling in love with him was the biggest lie of her life . . . she'd fallen early in the game. She'd known before he'd tricked her into being snowbound. The rat! She'd give anything to know what he was really up to with the mining companies.

Late that evening, she let herself into her dark apartment, clutching the contents of her mailbox in her teeth. The results of her assault on Marshall Field's spilled from her arms, and she had only two fingers free to turn the key.

The spill of light from the corner was a welcome sight. Ever since Chad had teased her about the lopsided shoe, she'd left the lamp on each morning to assure herself that a sign of life greeted her when she returned. The apartment seemed barren without his presence.

Only one item in her mail held any interest for her.

She eyed the tan envelope as if it might explode. Addressed in round, schoolteacherish script, the return address and postmark were instantly recognizable. She knew Chad's handwriting from his paperwork; this wasn't from him. Her nerves skittered as she loosened the tape-sealed flap. Why would anyone send an over-size envelope with a simple letter? A cream-colored cardboard rectangle and a folded circular fell to the floor as she slipped out the contents. She let them lie while she skipped to the signature on the single sheet. Erica.

The news was good. Daniel had Chad's blessings for art school; Chad was keeping Calico for Erica. Why did the workers in the restaurant today talk as if Calico had been sold? No mention was made of Chad buying out McDonald.

The next paragraph noted mournfully that Chad was thinner and extremely short-tempered. Aunt Clara worried about him, and she sent her love. "Thought you'd get a kick out of the enclosed. Chad promised to do this dumb thing last January, and now that the time has come, he's been trying to find a way to back out, so I reminded him this would be a great way to meet rich chicks. We've decided he should get mar-ried, and he might as well grab someone with money. He's a chauvinist, of course, and doesn't know how to admit he's wrong, but since he was such a pussycat about Daniel and me, we're hoping he's mellowing."

"Hah! I'll believe that when I see proof," Sabina commented as she put the letter aside and reached for the flyer.

Under the letterhead of a fund-raising group for Children's Hospital was an announcement of the auc-tion of "Dream Dates" with fifteen eligible area bach-elors. Chad's name was ninth on the list, which identified him as a financial/mining executive. "All proceeds tax-deductible. Personal checks, Mastercard and Visa accepted," was centered at the bottom of the fancifully decorated sheet.

The thick cream card served as both an invitation and a ticket to the auction. The black engraving blurred before Sabina's eyes. Her hands shook. Attempting to refocus her vision, she took a deep breath and exhaled to the count of ten in an effort to relax.

Flicking lights on as she went, Sabina ran to the kitchen to check her calendar. This coming Friday. She kicked off her shoes in front of the sink, recalling every moment they'd spent together. She pictured his clear, golden brown eyes gazing at her tenderly, the endearing creases that dented his cheeks when he grinned.

As if in a trance, she returned to her living room, vividly remembering their argument. He must have spoken with the twins soon after his return. The bull-headed fool must have discovered she was right within days of that encounter. Why had he taken so long to admit it? Why couldn't he just come to her and say, "I was wrong and you were right"?

Sabina realized Chad must know about the invitation in her hand. He'd teased her about being out of touch with what went on in Columbus. Did he want her to come see him being offered on the block like a prize chicken at the county fair and hope she'd bid for him? He was so infernally proud. It must have galled him to discover she knew the twins' real desires. And she couldn't fault his loyalty to others in his industry, even though he had to be aware not everyone shared his ethics. Did he know how to apologize?

Would he care enough to try?

"Why should I go to these lengths to talk to him? That idiot knows where I live." She threw the invitation on her desk, then picked it up and fingered the card thoughtfully.

Was she brave enough to attend?

Over the next two days, the question nagged at her. She changed her mind dozens of times, until she reached such a state of confusion that Friday morning she poured juice into the instant coffee she'd spooned into her cup.

"I wonder how much a weekend with him will cost?" she murmured, trying to ignore the little voice that answered, *It would be worth everything you own.* "Whatever he has planned, he better be ready to talk ... even if I have to handcuff him to his steering wheel."

The hotel lobby was crowded with expensively dressed women heading toward the ballroom. Wry remarks were punctuated by laughter as small groups of women crowded through the door and headed immediately for the cash bar.

Positive even a sniff of the cork from a wine bottle would complete her disintegration, Sabina bypassed a drink, opting for a tall glass of seltzer water. She needed her wits if she wanted to see this thing through.

She noticed she was one of the few women in attendance without a crowd of friends. How on earth

had Chad gotten himself into this thing? From the remarks she heard, a few of the women, at least those
around her, were as outspoken as any of the rough
miners she'd met, which was saying a lot.

"Lead me to the bidding. I can't wait to take a
sample home with me," a luscious redhead announced
to her friends as they crowded past Sabina.

Choosing a table in the back of the room seemed
safest. The bachelors were apparently going to walk
out a short runway attached to the small stage at the
opposite end. She couldn't take a chance on Chad
spotting her, in case she chickened out.

The tables were close to each other, and when the
bidding started she was grateful for the darkness at the
edges of the room. Never again would she accuse men
of being aggressive. Whistles and cheers came frequently from a table toward the front.

The flamboyant redhead triumphantly claimed the
engineer who was eighth on the program. Sabina's
temperature rose. Her cheeks felt flushed. The dates
offered ranged from a visit to Atlantic City casinos to
a flight to Hilton Head for golf and swimming. What
would Chad offer—a trip down the leaf slide?

"And now we come to item number nine on your
program, mining executive and bank president Chad
Peters. Chad hopes there is someone out there who
will share his love of music enough to bid a healthy
amount for charity. In return, he and his purchaser will
fly to Chicago to wine and dine in high style before
attending a performance of *The Marriage of Figaro*
by the Chicago Lyric Opera Company." The master

of ceremonies continued to tout Chad's eligibility and accomplishments, but his words were lost on Sabina.

Chad was offering her dream trip! She'd been set up. The slimy lowlife was dangling her own bait in front of her!

When the red mist in front of her eyes cleared, Sabina started to laugh. Was this the only way he could bring himself to apologize? If he would go this far in public, he really did care, didn't he? But still, that was *her* special treat!

"You'll pay for this," she murmured, determined to see him squirm. "I'm your only way out." The man owed her another apology.

The flowery introduction came to an end, and Chad stepped through the curtains, drawing an appreciative murmur and a chorus of wolf whistles from the crowd, which had become increasingly uninhibited. At the sight of him, heat spread through Sabina as if her blood had warmed. She definitely hadn't imagined his effect on her. Even across the ballroom, all her senses were in place and functioning overtime.

So far, the men had worn conventional tuxedos or business suits. Chad had taken formal dress a step further. His black tuxedo jacket lay across his shoulders as only a custom-tailored coat could. The tucked shirt was so white it looked like an ad for laundry detergent, the contrast with the tartan bow tie and cummerbund accentuating its pristine state.

Below the formal gear he wore the tightest, most faded jeans Sabina had ever seen. They fit like a second skin, prompting moaning sounds from someone to her left. Heavy steel-toed boots were laced to mid calf, accentuating his rugged masculinity, and a yellow hard hat tilted low on his forehead at an arrogant angle, nearly covering his eyes. A come-hither grin creased his lips.

The auctioneer cut smoothly into the hubbub. ''Do I hear a bid?''

Sabina held her breath as a heavyset blond started the bidding at $500, but the amount climbed fast and furiously, in fifty- and one-hundred-dollar increments, while Sabina watched Chad's expression. The devilish grin never faltered, but she saw the slight movement of his head each time a new voice entered the auction. He seemed to be listening intently to each bidder, as if searching for a familiar voice. She sat silent, sipping her seltzer. He could squirm a little longer.

The blond persisted, commenting to her friends, ''I'm going to spend everything I've saved if I have to.''

Sabina wondered if her own savings would be enough.

Chad's nerves tightened. Sabina was here, wasn't she? Erica had assured him there was no way she could resist. But what did an eighteen-year-old girl know? If she was out there, why wasn't she bidding? Dear heaven. This looked like the beginning of a disaster. If someone other than Sabina bought him, he wasn't sure he would survive the weekend. Only willpower kept him from fleeing the room. Where was Sabina?

* * *

Sabina was enjoying the growing fear on the face of the helpless auction prize on the stage. His male pride deserved just a tad more battering.

Suddenly she realized the bidding war had slowed. She'd been so immersed in her plans for revenge that she hadn't been paying attention.

The blond shouted, "$2,350. And worth every penny." Everyone else had dropped out.

Projecting her voice, Sabina called, "$2,999.99."

At the sound of her voice, Sabina watched Chad push the hard hat up from his eyebrows and attempt a casual survey of the room. The areas around the edge were in shadow, while a haze floated in the harsh light illuminating the small stage. She wondered whether he was kicking himself for being roped into this thing, and how long it would take him to spit out an apology.

"Any more bids, ladies? Don't let that last jump hold you back." The perspiring auctioneer did his best, but Sabina's bid had quieted the crowd. "Going once. Going twice. Gone! Will the lady in the back of the room come forward and claim her purchase?"

Sabina took her time. She drained her glass of seltzer water, freshened her lipstick, and made her leisurely way between the tables. Schooling her expression carefully, she looked up to make sure Chad was watching. Satisfied by his intent stare, she moved as if she had all day.

The odd bid had triggered an excited buzz of speculation. The crowd applauded as Sabina climbed the carpeted treads to the stage. The tiny frown etching Chad's forehead pleased her.

The frown deepened, then faded. She was sure he realized he would have to grovel. *Back to square one, big boy*. Nerves made her throat tight, but she refused to back down. She hadn't slept or eaten properly for three weeks.

As if sensing undercurrents, the auctioneer made quick work of asking Sabina her name and bundling them off to the cashier to transact the real purpose of the evening—payment. Sabina held Chad's arm with an impersonal touch, even though she wanted to clutch him tightly.

She signed the check with a flourish, dropping the pale blue slip of paper in front of the fashionably gowned cashier as if it were nothing, when in fact that morning she'd emptied her savings account, transferring $3,000 to checking. In response to the woman's effusive thanks, she said airily, "This is *such* a good cause."

Her insides quivered from two emotions: sheer excitement at his nearness, and fear she would cave in before she heard an apology. She couldn't think of a thing to say as they walked down the hall.

At the elevator, Chad leaned close to murmur in her ear, "Ninety-nine cents! This isn't a discount store, Sabina."

His teasing revived her spirit. "Really? I thought it was a beef market. Steak is always priced at a cent below the dollar to make the buyer think he's getting a bargain." The hall was deserted; as the elevator light glowed red she stepped back and looked him over. "You're prime stuff. That big blond was itching to get her hands on you. I heard her say so."

The silence during their descent was deafening.

After the revolving door coughed them onto the street, Sabina said coolly, "I drove. If you want to meet me at my place, we can make our arrangements."

Nodding acquiescence, Chad set out in the opposite direction, ignoring the curious glances his attire drew from passersby. Walking rapidly, with his shoulders hunched, hands in pockets, his thoughts were humbling company. When Sabina had finally called the winning bid, he had nearly fainted with relief. The last three weeks had been a nightmare.

Chad wasn't accustomed to being wrong, and even less accustomed to admitting it. Erica's suggestion of offering Sabina's dream weekend as bait had seemed like a good idea at the time, but things seemed to have gone awry. Erica was convinced Sabina would look on the invitation as a sign he wanted to apologize. From what he'd seen of her actions since the auction, he wasn't so sure. At the very least, she meant to make him eat crow.

Locating his car, Chad climbed in and twisted his key in the ignition, then sat listening to the banked power of the engine. If she wanted to see him swallow his pride, he would do it. He refused to think defeat.

By the time Chad arrived, Sabina had kicked off her shoes and started a pot of coffee. Strong coffee. She took several deep breaths before she answered the door. At the sight of him framed in her doorway, she felt her heart beat in her throat.

"I nearly sent out a search party to locate my investment," she said, determined to be difficult. He'd removed the hard hat, and his hair curled damply over his forehead. Sabina had never seen anything so appealing in her life.

He responded softly, "Don't push, Sabina. This is hard enough as it is."

Leaving him to close the door, Sabina crossed the room to distance herself. She couldn't weaken, no matter how much she wanted to. "It shouldn't be that difficult. If Erica hadn't sent me a ticket, I wouldn't have known you were on the block." She played with the silk flowers in a crystal vase. "If someone had topped my bid, I would have had to drop out."

"You can always borrow from your friendly banker."

The flowers slipped from her fingers. Chad picked up the scattered blossoms before she could reach them, and stood before her, running the stems through his fingers. She snatched them from him and turned her back while she stuffed them haphazardly into the vase. Things weren't going as she'd anticipated. "No, I couldn't. That was *my* weekend you offered to anyone with the money to buy it."

Turning back, she said angrily, "You almost squandered *my* dream."

"Sabina, I'm sorry . . ."

She drew a deep breath and looked up at him, her

hands on her hips. This was the confrontation she sought. "Why did you have to go to such lengths to see me?"

Suddenly, groveling wasn't out of the question. Chad would do anything to remove the hurt in her eyes. "Because I was wrong . . . I didn't trust you. Because I have some ingrained notions that get me into trouble now and then." For the first time in his life, his voice cracked with the sincerity of a man desperately in love. "Because I love you."

For some reason, his declaration seemed to confuse her. "So you put me through this . . . this travesty?"

"All right. I was a jerk, and I had a whole truckload of false pride that wouldn't allow me to simply come and beg." His voice faltered. "I couldn't imagine admitting there were any lapses in my judgment, or that I'd jumped to the conclusion that you only pretended my arguments had convinced you to take a broader view. That you'd shut down McDonald out of spite."

He edged closer. "Sabina, I'm willing to spend the rest of my life apologizing for that if you'll let me. I want you. I'm not sure I can live without you."

Sabina turned to fuss with the flowers again, but not before he saw the relief in her eyes.

"I love you, Sabina. And I think you love me, or we wouldn't be here."

Sabina turned to face him. "You manipulated me. Now that I have you, I'm not sure why I should want you."

"When I left this afternoon, Aunt Clara told me to use the sense God gave a goose, whatever that means.

She and the twins think you'll protect me from that pack of women I'm supposed to have at my heels twenty-four hours a day.''

The older woman's dry, no-nonsense way of speaking played back through Sabina's mind, bringing tears of laughter to her eyes, and breaking her composure. Shoulders shaking, she lowered her eyes. ''You'd still be a chauvinist.''

''I'm doing my best to reform. What else can I do to make you say yes?''

Humility was the last thing she'd ever expected to hear in his voice. She couldn't resist one last caveat. ''You'll have to give up encouraging all those women.''

''That should be easy. They only exist in the imaginations of people with nothing else to talk about.''

''Your reputation has to be built on something,'' Sabina teased. She knew how much it had cost him to apologize. He wasn't accustomed to being wrong; he was clearly uncomfortable with the state.

A fine line of perspiration had broken out on his upper lip. ''I don't know what else I can do. I love you, Sabina.''

If she didn't touch him soon, she would expire from need. Smiling, Sabina laid her arms around his neck. ''Kiss me. Kiss me very hard. After about fifty years, you might convince me.''

Chad nearly shouted with relief. Instead, he folded her against him as if afraid she would break. When he finally kissed her, it was a kiss of commitment, rather than passion. Chad realized he had never before kissed a woman with so much emotion.

Moments later, Sabina drew back, the love in her eyes making them glow like large sapphires. "I love you, Chad. Even though you said I was wrong about McDonald, I knew you wouldn't approve of what he'd done. I could only hope you'd be as fair as I believed you to be—that you'd find out for yourself."

Clutching her as if he were afraid she'd be snatched away, Chad admitted, "I was an idiot to suspect you'd punish one person to get even with the whole industry." He pulled her closer. "You've been exposed to my temper and now to my distrust. Will you believe me when I promise I've learned my lesson?"

She snuggled against him, and rubbed her nose lightly against the pristine linen of his shirt. "You need more practice. With the right teacher, you could learn a lot about equality."

"Are you volunteering for the job?"

Tugging him backward toward the bed, Sabina teased, "Is this an interview or a proposal?"

"Both. Besides, you have to marry me. I've already bought your wedding gift."

Shaken by the sudden intensity of his expression, Sabina could manage only a faint echo. "Wedding gift?"

"I'm sure Erica told you we weren't selling Calico. She left out something. I bought McDonald's mess. I want those abandoned sites reclaimed, and I thought you'd enjoy doing the job." Smiling, he continued.

"But you can't unless you're my wife. Call it more of a bribe than a gift."

Sabina's eyes sparkled with excitement. "Don't you know this state employee doesn't accept bribes?"

"You could quit your job. Then we wouldn't be on opposite sides of the fence," he cajoled.

The thought of working to salvage the abandoned sites excited Sabina. Restoring those eroded scars would be a privilege. No other gift could have demonstrated his love and understanding more. "I don't need a bribe to marry you, Chad." She didn't care if he heard the tears in her voice. They were tears of joy. She wondered if his happiness was singing in his veins as it was in hers.

"There's a catch. You'll have to manage both mining companies . . . at least till Erica's ready to take over Calico."

Sabina grinned, then leaned forward to rest her forehead against his. "Fair enough." She sealed her promise with a kiss.

Sighing as if the weight of eternity had just been lifted from his shoulders, Chad savored her closeness while the reality of the future sank in. "We made it, Sabina. In spite of everything, we made it."

Sabina smiled shakily. "I'm not sure I know how to return love, Chad. No one ever taught me how. Please don't let me fail you. I promise to do my best to make you happy. Forever."

"That's supposed to be *my* line. If we both do our best, we can't lose."

"What are the odds at the mine?" she teased.

He returned her grin, then drew her close. "Jonas said all the bets were on you."

"I'm *really* going to enjoy working with that crew," Sabina announced into the pristine tucks of his shirt.